The FRYEBURG CHRONICLES

The FRYEBURG CHRONICLES

After the Battle

BOOK V

JUNE O'DONAL

Copyright © 2019 by June O'Donal.

Library of Congress Control Number:		2019913345
ISBN:	Hardcover	978-1-7960-5733-1
	Softcover	978-1-7960-5732-4
	eBook	978-1-7960-5731-7

All rights reserved. No part of this book may be reproduced or transmitted in any form or by any means, electronic or mechanical, including photocopying, recording, or by any information storage and retrieval system, without permission in writing from the copyright owner.

This is a work of fiction. Names, characters, places and incidents either are the product of the author's imagination or are used fictitiously, and any resemblance to any actual persons, living or dead, events, or locales is entirely coincidental.

Scripture quotations marked KJV are from the Holy Bible, King James Version (Authorized Version). First published in 1611. Quoted from the KJV Classic Reference Bible, Copyright © 1983 by The Zondervan Corporation.

Print information available on the last page.

Rev. date: 09/17/2019

To order additional copies of this book, contact:
Xlibris
1-888-795-4274
www.Xlibris.com
Orders@Xlibris.com
800841

"And if a house be divided against itself, that house cannot stand." Mark 3:25

"A house divided against itself cannot stand. I believe this government cannot endure, permanently half slave and half free. I do not expect the Union to be dissolved—I do not expect the house to fall—but I do expect it will cease to be divided. It will become all one thing, or all the other." Abraham Lincoln June 16, 1858

In Loving Memory

Beatrice Seavey 1944- 2019
My aunt, "big sister", friend and mentor
Her life and faith are the inspiration for Daniel Miller.

THE FRYEBURG CHRONICLES BOOK V
AFTER THE BATTLE

TABLE OF CONTENTS

Acknowledgments xi
Historical Fiction: What is Historical and What is Fiction? xiii
The Miller Family Tree xv
American Political Parties from 1790's - 1860 xvii
Map of Fryeburg Maine xix
Map of Gettysburg xx

Part I Fryeburg

    I.   Election Day 1
    II.   Snowstorms and Headlines 14
    III.   War! 23
    IV.   Enlistment 30
    V.   The Home Front 42

Part II Gettysburg

    VI.   The Schaeffer Family 52
    VII.   The Gunther Family 57
    VIII.   The Reporter 66
    IX.   The Arrival 75
    X.   The Search 83
    XI.   Camp Letterman 97

Part III Fryeburg

    XII.   The Return 104
    XIII.   A Long Row to Hoe 112
    XIV.   A New Beginning 125

XV.	Discovery in Gettysburg	132
XVI.	A Tale of Two Homecomings	138
XVII.	The Adjustments	149
XVIII.	Secrets	161
XIX.	Andersonville Prison Letters	170
XX.	War's End	187
XXI.	The Reason	196

Discussion Questions 203
Fryeburg Landmarks 209
The Fryeburg Chronicles Own the Entire Series 213
End Notes 215
Bibliography 221

Acknowledgments

Writing is a solitary endeavor. Researching requires a village. I am indebted to the Fryeburg Historical Society for access to historical records in their research library and their permission to reproduce historic photographs. The description of the Miller's Traveling Apothecary wagon is based upon the Rosenbloom peddler wagon owned and displayed by the Society.

My gratitude to the Fryeburg Public Library for the numerous interlibrary loan books.

Herbalist, Carol Felice has been invaluable in sharing her knowledge about herbal remedies and providing recipes.

My husband, Wayne, designed the maps of Fryeburg, Maine and Gettysburg, Pennsylvania incorporating fictional locations with historic locations relevant to the novel.

Several people contributed to the front cover. Thank you, Bob Pierce, and the 3rd Regiment of Maine Civil War Reenactors who held an encampment on the property of the Fryeburg Historical Society on August 17-18. They generously and enthusiastically lent me their artifacts and assisted in the photo shoot. The talented Terri Tomlin of the Fryeburg Historical Society designed and created the rag dolls and assisted in staging the photo shoot. My son, Timothy O'Donal, assisted with the cover design.

Thank you to my patient family who has listened about the Miller family, aka "mom's imaginary friends", since 2010 when I began writing Book I. My always insightful daughter, Perry Hopkins, made some great suggestions which added depth to the plot and character development.

Above all, thank you to my faithful readers who have encouraged and supported me from the beginning. I am sorry that it took three years to complete Book V. Cancer recovery slowed me down but didn't stop me! Now on to Book VI…

Historical Fiction: What is Historical and What is Fiction?

Fryeburg, Maine, established in 1762, the earliest town in the White Mountain region, is located along the Saco River in western Maine at the New Hampshire border. Col. Joseph Frye was granted this isolated township for his heroic service in the French and Indian War. It became a prosperous agricultural community with lumber mills, shop keepers, quarries, tanneries, and churches. The Fryeburg Academy and the Fryeburg Fair have played an important role in its history.

The extended Miller family are fictional characters. Peter and Rachel Evans' General Store is fictional, although there was an Evans General Store in a different time period and location. I have included a modified map of Fryeburg depicting the fictional and the historic buildings and photographs of landmarks depicted in this novel. Fryeburg history is filled with members of the Weston, Osgood, Bradley and Hastings families. When both first and last names are used, I am referring to a historic person. When Mr. or Mrs. last name only is used, it is a fictional person within the family.

Monroe Quint was born in Conway, NH in 1844 and served in the 17th Regiment of Maine. The following physical description was written at the time of his enlistment: "hazel eyes, light hair and light complexion, 5'8" in height." In May 1863 he fought in the Battle of Chancellorsville in Virginia and was awarded the Kearny Cross. He also fought in the Battle of Gettysburg. The events of his life depicted on July 3 are true.

Gettysburg, Pennsylvania was a prosperous city with 2,400 residents, a new courthouse, several churches of different denominations, a seminary and many shops and businesses before

July 1, 1863. Today it is remembered for the bloody battle fought from July 1 – 3 in 1863.

Every citizen from infant to elderly was impacted by this devastating battle. The Schaeffer, Gunther and Peterson families are fictional characters illustrating the hardships experienced by many women, children, farmers, shopkeepers and the vulnerable elderly. To learn more about the lives of the civilians in Gettysburg, please refer to the bibliography at the end of the book.

All minor historic characters are named with both first and last names. Fictional characters are not named or are called by first name only.

Camp Letterman, named after Surgeon Major Jonathon Letterman Medical Director of the Army of the Potomac, served as a military hospital near the Gettysburg Battlefield to treat more than 14,000 Union and 6,800 Confederate wounded soldiers.

U.S. Sanitation Commission was a private relief agency created by federal legislation to support sick and wounded soldiers of the Union Army during the American Civil War. Its purpose was to promote clean and healthy conditions in Army camps, staff field hospitals, raise money, provide supplies, and work to educate the military and government on matters of health and sanitation.

U.S. Christian Commission was an organization that furnished volunteers, donated supplies, medical services, and religious literature to Union troops during the American Civil War. It combined religious support with social services and recreational activities.

Sharpshooters Champion marksman Hiram C. Berdan of New York, authorized to raise a regiment of sharpshooters for Federal service, began recruiting competitions in the summer of 1861.

17th Regiment of Maine. Although the regiment did fight in Gettysburg where many soldiers died, they did not fight near the fictional Gunther farm. I took a literary license in relocating the Millers, Darian and the 17th Regiment there so they could interact with the Gunther family there. The 17th Regiment fought at the Wheatfield on July 2, 1863, the second day of battle. After their losses, the regiment was moved to the middle of the line at Cemetery Ridge.

Miller Family Tree

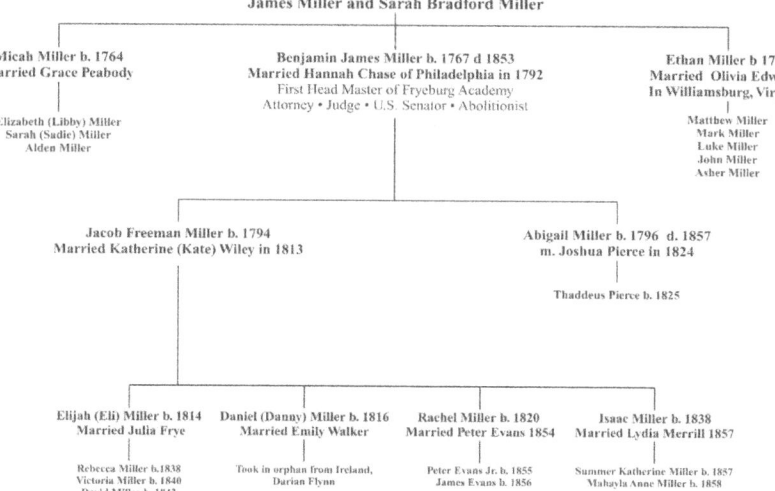

American Political Parties from 1790's - 1860

The Federalists Party (1790's - 1820's) Led by Alexander Hamilton, John Adams and John Jay, it was the first American political party. It called for a strong national government that promoted economic growth, fostered friendly relationships with Great Britain and opposition to Revolutionary France. The party controlled the federal government until 1801, when it was overwhelmed by the Democratic-Republicans.

The Democratic-Republican Party, in opposition to the Federalist Party, contended that government did not have the right to adopt additional powers to fulfill its duties under the Constitution. It was formed by Thomas Jefferson and James Madison in 1792 to oppose the centralizing policies of the new Federalist Party.

The Democratic Party, preceded by Democratic-Republican party, was founded by Andrew Jackson and Martin Van Buren in **1828. Jacksonian Democrats** championed greater rights for the common man and was opposed to any signs of aristocracy in the nation. The Democratic Party split in two over the slavery question.

The Whig Party was organized in 1834 by political opponents of President Andrew Jackson to contest Jacksonian Democrats nationally and in the states. Henry Clay was their most prominent leader. Yet during the party's brief life, it managed to win support from diverse economic groups in all sections and to hold their own in presidential elections. In 1852, as slavery's expansion became the great issue of American politics, the Whigs suffered a drastic decline in popularity.

The Free-Soil Party was an American political party that only survived the 1848 and 1852 presidential elections. Essentially a single-issue reform party, it was dedicated to stopping the spread of slavery to new states and territories in the West. It attracted a very dedicated following. In 1854 it merged with the Republican Party.

The Republican Party grew out of opposition to the Kansas–Nebraska Act, which was signed into law by President Franklin Pierce in 1854. Its founders included abolitionists, Conscience Whigs and Free-Soil Democrats.

Parties in the 1860 Election

The Federalist, Free-Soil and Whig Parties no longer existed. Both the Whigs in the North, called the Conscience Whigs and the Free-Soil Party merged into the Republican Party.

In the South the Whigs reorganized themselves as the **Constitutional Union Party.**

The Democratic Party split over the slavery question into **Moderate Democrats** in the North and the **Proslavery Democrats** of the South.

Republican Party – Abraham Lincoln

Constitutional Union Party – John Bell

Moderate Democrat – Stephen Douglas

Pro-Slavery Southern faction of the Democratic Party – John Breckinridge.

Map of Fryeburg Maine
1850

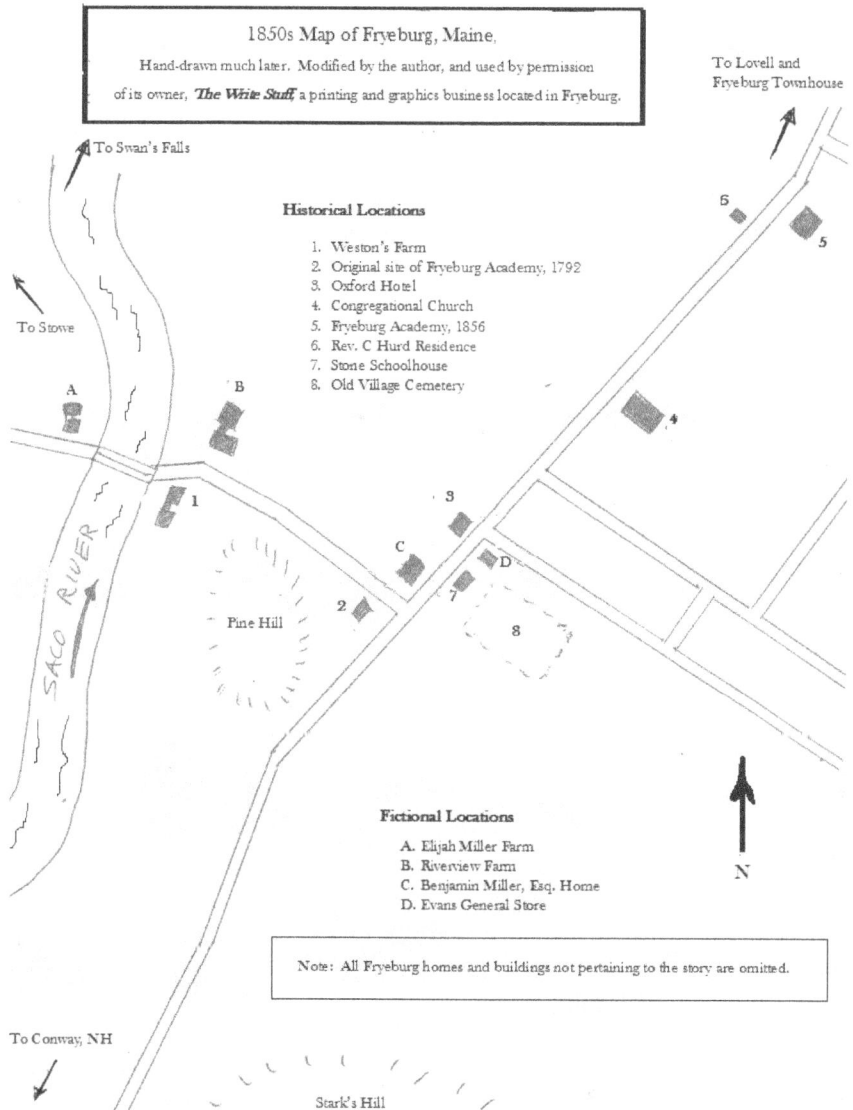

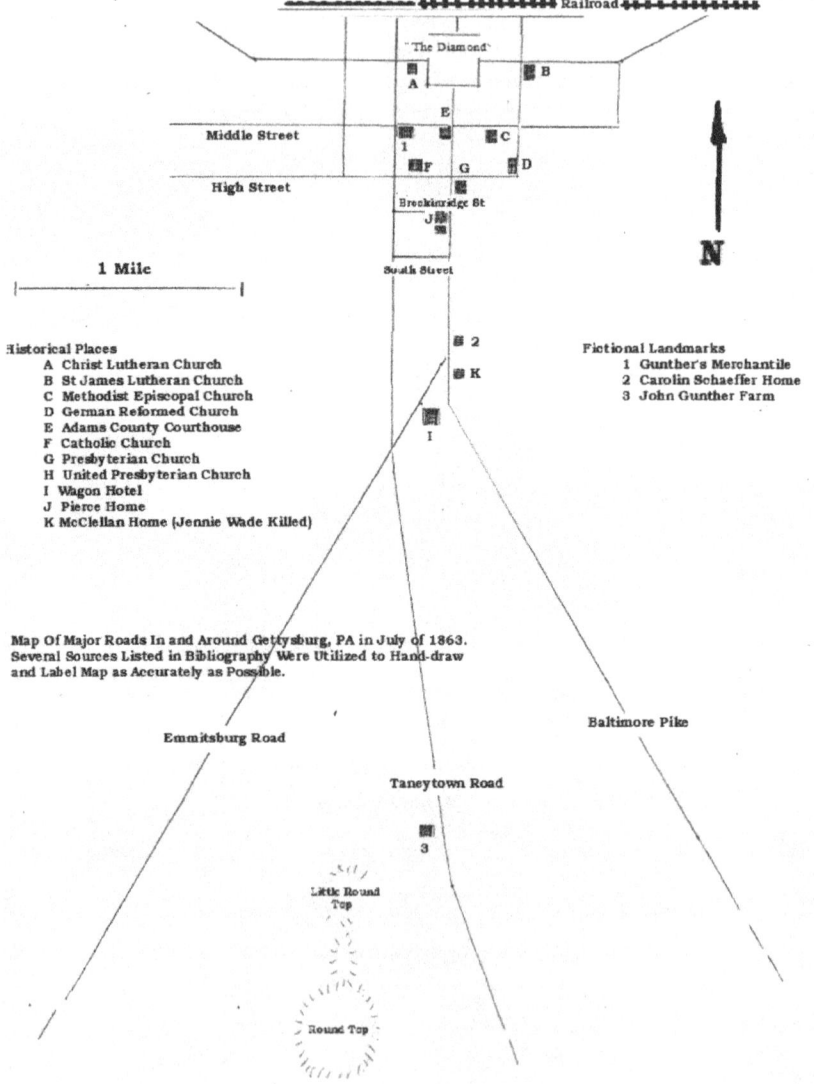

I

Election Day

Fryeburg, Maine November 6, 1860

It was an ordinary morning of an extraordinary day. Dawn was breaking over the modest home of Elijah Miller on the bank of the Saco River. Eli and his sixteen- year-old son David drank their first cup of coffee by the light of an oil lamp and the warmth of the cook stove. As the bacon sizzled and the eggs fried, David asked, "Pa, who are you going to vote for?"

"I have given this a great deal of thought. I have often wondered who my grandfather would vote for. He was first a Federalist and then a Whig. But today neither party exists."

"I remember Senator Miller sitting at his desk in his big office filled with books. One day he told me he wanted me to grow up to become President of the United States. He was certain I would do a better job than Millard Fillmore."

Eli burst out laughing. "What did you tell him?"

"I told him that first I would be a farmer and when my son was old enough to take over the farm, then I would be President."

"Good answer," Eli approved.

"Of course, I did not take him seriously at the time. However, I have begun to consider it. The Senator grew up on a farm just like I did. He learned at home. He did not have the advantage of attending Fryeburg Academy like I do. I could read and study all your grandfather's law books and then serve as an apprentice to Attorney Hastings. This would give me a solid foundation. Perhaps I could be a selectman like my Uncle Caleb Frye and then a state senator."

Eli beamed with pride at his only son.

"David, I am pleased you have remembered that you are also a descendant of Joseph Frye, the founder of this town. He fought gallantly in both the French and Indian War and the War for Independence," his mother, Julia Frye Miller reminded.

In turn Eli asked his son, "If you could vote today, who would you vote for?"

"This is an interesting election with four candidates. The Democratic Party split in two over the slavery question. Stephen Douglas from the North is running as a moderate Democrat. He thinks we can keep compromising. John Breckinridge from the South is on the Slavery platform.[1]

The demise of the Whig Party led to two new parties. The Republican Party came from remnants of the Free-Soil Party and the Conscientious Whigs and many other local elements unified to confront the Democrats.[2] They nominated Abraham Lincoln from Illinois. In the South the Whigs reorganized themselves as the Constitutional Union Party with John Bell as their nominee.[3]

I would rule out the two southern candidates which leaves Douglas and Lincoln. Douglas is a grand orator, but I would vote for Lincoln," David decided.

"You know the South threatens to secede if Lincoln is elected," Eli warned.

"Lincoln says that a house divided against itself cannot stand. It will become all one thing or all the other."

Eli nodded. "Did you learn this at Fryeburg Academy?"

"No. I learned this from talking with Aunt Rachel," he grinned.

"Well, my sister is a strong willed, opinionated woman!"

"Just like her older brother, dear," Julia laughed as she took the biscuits out of the oven, dished the bacon and eggs on three plates in one efficient motion. She placed breakfast on the table, poured herself a cup of coffee, and buttered the warm biscuits before taking her place beside her husband.

"I told Aunt Rachel I will give women the vote when I become President."

"Good grief," Eli shook his head.

"Your sisters, aunts and I will all vote for your reelection," Julia promised.

The Millers celebrated four holidays: Christmas, Easter, Fourth of July and Election Day. David and his best friend, Monroe Quint, would not be attending Fryeburg Academy today. Latin, mathematics and history would have to wait, for they would accompany their fathers to the Fryeburg Town House to watch the men vote. The extended Miller family would celebrate the occasion by sharing the noon meal at River View Farm, the family homestead.

"Thank you for breakfast, Julia. David, do you know how fortunate we are that your mother is even a better cook than Nana. Make sure you marry a woman who can cook," Eli advised.

"Aunt Rachel says I should marry a woman who can think for herself."

"Your father married a woman who can do both," Julia settled the matter. "After breakfast could you please bring the food to the farm in the wagon. I will walk over later."

They carried a pot of stew, three apple pies, four loaves of bread, and three jugs of cider to the wagon and headed over the covered bridge to the farm. Eli, the fourth-generation farmer, always loved the sprawling, white farmhouse with the attached red barn. He grew up in this house listening to stories how his great-grandfather, James, a minister from Boston emigrated to Fryeburg, purchased acres of fertile soil and built a humble two room house with a loft in the 1760's. He raised three sons here until a young, wealthy girl from Boston unexpectedly arrived at the family's doorstep during the Revolutionary War.

Grace Peabody appeared with wagons of furniture, clothing, bedding, china and gold coins sewn into her petticoats. She designed the formal dining room, front parlor and two downstairs bedrooms to accommodate her possessions. The three Miller sons slept on the second floor. Her gold coins paid the workers' wages. Young Grace, who married Micah Miller, became Eli's favorite great-aunt Grace Miller. She also lived in this home until her death in 1857 at the age of ninety.

At one time this home was filled with four generations of Millers; now only Eli's elderly parents lived here. He understood the time would come when he, Julia and David would move in to care for his parents and to take over the property. In turn, David would care for Julia and him in their old age and inherit the farm. Life was good in Fryeburg, Maine in 1860.

* * *

It was still dark when Eli's sister, Rachel Miller Evans, quietly closed the door to their second-floor apartment and descended the stairs to ready their store for a busy day. She would have two uninterrupted hours before her two sons arose and prepared for school. Evans General Store was centrally located in Fryeburg Village between the brick Fryeburg Academy and the stone Village School House, across the street from the bustling Oxford Hotel and a half mile from her parents' peaceful farm.

"Good morning," her husband, Peter greeted. He had already started the potbelly stove in the center of the store and lit several lamps. "It promises to be a busy day."

After voting, many of the men who lived on isolated farms would stock up on winter supplies before returning home. The regulars would also stop by to argue about politics and do a little shopping. Rachel was sorting the U.S. mail when she exclaimed in exasperation, "It is simply not fair that women are not allowed to vote!"

This was not the first time the couple had this conversation. "I agree. You know much more about politics than most women."

"I know much more about politics than most men," she corrected. "My grandfather taught me just as much about politics and government as my brothers. Yet today they will vote while I am denied the privilege. No, the right to vote."

"If you could vote today, who would you vote for?" he wisely steered the conversation to another topic.

"This election is so different from the previous ones because it is no longer Whig versus Democrat. There are now four nominees from four political parties. Naturally I have ruled out the two Southern nominees. I have spent months reading the papers," she nodded to the stack of newspapers on the counter. "I would vote for the Republican Abraham Lincoln," she stated emphatically.

* * *

The sun was rising over the cabin at Miller Lumber Mill at Walker's Falls on the Saco River. Proprietor, Daniel Miller, and his wife, Emily, were dressed in their Sunday best. Twenty-two-year-old Darian Flynn climbed down the ladder from the loft where he slept. The orphan, who escaped the Great Hunger in Ireland in 1848, lived with Daniel's grandparents for a few years before moving in with them and working at the mill.

"Are you ready for the big day?" Daniel asked as he poured himself a cup of tea.

Darian's smile was his response. He was like a son to this childless, middle-aged couple. Today they were going to visit Attorney Hastings' office to make Darian a business partner with 40% ownership of the mill. Now an American citizen, he would accompany Daniel to the Town House, where he would vote for the first time. After voting, they would celebrate Election Day with Daniel's parents and siblings.

After a hurried breakfast, Emily placed two baskets of children's clothing in the wagon and the three of them headed west toward the village.

* * *

Eli and David placed all the food on the long, pine trestle table in the farmhouse's kitchen. Kate Miller was baking a ham, peeling potatoes and chopping carrots. "Mama, this is enough food to feed the town of Fryeburg!"

The elderly woman smiled, for nothing made her happier than having the family together. A decade ago, the family was larger and ate together regularly. Over time, the oldest generation passed away while the youngest generation left home to begin families of their own. "A special occasion deserves a special meal," she proclaimed.

With each passing year, David looked more like Eli while Eli looked more like Jacob. Three generations of Miller men had curly hair and gray eyes inherited from Jacob's mother, Hannah Miller. David's hair was dark brown, Eli's brown with wisps of gray and Jacob's silver. "Life is good," Kate thought gratefully.

"Are you playing hooky from school today?" Jacob teased his grandson.

"No, sir. I mean yes, sir. I will be coming to the Town House with you today."

"You know, my father was born a British subject back in 1767. He always told me there is no greater responsibility for a man than to vote."

"For a man perhaps. But not for a woman," Kate reminded her husband.

"Have you been talking to Rachel?" Eli accused his mother.

"No, your sister has been talking to me," she replied tartly. "I hope I live to see the day when my daughter or my granddaughters have the right to vote."

"Well, no one will vote today if we do not get the chores done first," Jacob winked at his wife and stood up to leave.

Three generations of farmers milked the cows, fed the livestock and collected the eggs. "Grandpa, you go back inside and warm up. I will finish," David offered.

Jacob could rest assured knowing after he was gone, the farm would be in capable hands.

"Do you think you could convince Nana to give me a slice of apple pie?"

"I think I could convince your grandmother to give you an entire apple pie!" Jacob chuckled.

Upon the completion of the chores, Eli and David reentered the house. The woodstoves in the front parlor and the dining room were warming the house as the November sunshine streamed through the windows. An entire apple pie, plates, silverware and a pot of coffee awaited them on the dining room table.

"Thank you, Nana," David grinned as he sliced a piece for his grandfather. Suddenly the back door opened, and a disheveled Isaac Miller rushed in.

"Nice of you to show up," Eli rolled his eyes at his youngest brother.

Ignoring the comment, Isaac turned to Jacob, "Pa, I am sorry I overslept again. The girls were up all night and…" his voice trailed off.

Kate bit her tongue for she was determined not to be an interfering mother-in-law. By the ages of two and three, her granddaughters should be sleeping in their own beds through the night. Her son and daughter-in-law did not provide the children with discipline and structure. "Have you had any breakfast?" she asked knowing the answer.

"No, Mama."

"Well, I will fix you something to hold you over until lunch."

Eli sighed. At the age of twenty-two Isaac was a generation younger than his siblings. "Spoiled mama's boy," he thought in disgust. This happy-go-lucky child grew into an aimless, young man. He was not inclined to work for his brother at the sawmill nor for his father on the farm. Four years ago, he had quickly altered his plans to attend Bowdoin College when he unexpectedly inherited his grandfather's gracious home on Main Street. To his family's surprise, he married a young woman from a questionable family and two babies soon followed.

"David, no school today?" Isaac asked his nephew.

"It is Election Day," he explained.

"It is? Election Day is today?"

Eli shook his head. Maybe his sister had a point.

* * *

Attorney Hastings shook Darian's hand. "Congratulations, Mr. Flynn. I wish you and Mr. Miller much continued success."

"Thank you, sir. Only in America could an immigrant with nothing but the clothes on his back become a self-sufficient businessman."

As their wagon passed Isaac's house on the corner of Main Street and River Street, Emily requested, "Please stop by the back door. I would like to deliver these baskets of clothing to Lydia."

Daniel looked skeptically at his wife.

"It is only for a quick visit. If Lydia does not wish to have company, I will simply drop off the clothing and walk to the farm."

She knocked on the unlocked kitchen door. Receiving no response, she hesitantly stepped in and called, "Hello. Lydia, it is Emily." She looked around at the kitchen in dismay. Dirty dishes were piled on the kitchen table and in the soapstone sink. Dirty clothes were strewn throughout the dining room.

Lydia, still dressed in her night clothes, quickly descended the back stairs. "What are you doing here?" she demanded.

"I was on my way to the farm and I wanted to drop off these dresses for the girls."

"They are asleep. They just fell asleep a half hour ago." She blushed in shame at the sight of her home.

"Have you been up all night? Gracious, go back to bed and get some sleep. I will wash a few dishes. When the girls awaken, we can try them on," she suggested. "We are all invited for lunch at the farm."

Exhaustion outweighed her pride and Lydia reluctantly returned upstairs.

Emily spent the next two hours, washing dishes, scrubbing the kitchen, sweeping the floors and dusting the furniture. She gathered the dirty clothing by the back door with intention to wash them at home the next day. She heard little bare feet patter down the stairs.

"Bekfist?" Three-year-old Summer Katherine shyly asked her aunt.

"Breakfast, please," Emily corrected.

"Bekfist, pease," Summer repeated.

"Good girl, Summer," Emily picked up her niece, wrapped her in a wool shawl and placed her in the chair closest to the stove. "Would you like some oatmeal?"

"Yes, pease."

Moments later two-year-old Mahayla Anne came crying down the stairs and stared at Emily.

"Bekfist? Sit and be warm," Summer invited.

After the sisters had eaten, Emily showed the collection of dresses to the two excited girls. "Now pick one out to wear to Nana and Grandpa's house." They decided to wear matching blue wool dresses trimmed in white lace.

Emily had the girls' hair combed and neatly braided with new blue ribbons, when Lydia reappeared. "You look like little princesses," the young mother exclaimed clutching her shawl. She looked around at the kitchen and began to cry.

Emily diverted her attention. "Lydia, you may not believe this, but I was once your size," laughed her matronly sister-in-law. "Here are some of my favorite dresses. I accept the fact that I will never fit in them again. Nothing fancy, mind you. But you could wear them around the house."

"Emily, they are beautiful! I cannot accept them," she protested.

"They will only take up space in my armoire and remind me of the weight I gained. Go ahead, try one on and you can wear it to lunch."

* * *

All five of the Miller men climbed into the wagon. As they traveled up Main Street, Peter ran out of the store waving to them to stop. "Do you have room for one more?"

"The more the merrier," Jacob invited jovially as Peter hopped in the back of the wagon with Daniel, Darian, and Isaac. They slowly drove past the Oxford Hotel, several homes and businesses, the newly built brick Fryeburg Academy and bore left onto the road to Lovell.

There was some controversy in 1857 when the town discussed the location of the new Town House. Residents of the Village believed it was only logical to build it where most of the population resided. The farmers in the out-lying areas of Fryeburg Harbor, North Fryeburg and East Fryeburg wanted a more central location. The Town House was finally built in Center Fryeburg near Joseph Frye's original homestead.

"Pa, I am sorry that we cannot get any closer. I could drop you off by the door," Eli offered as the wagon neared the crowded Town House. Carriages, wagons and horses lined both sides of the narrow, dirt road.

"Nonsense!" Jacob protested. "It is a perfect day for a brisk walk. It will get my blood moving," he said cheerfully as he pulled up the collar of his brown, wool coat. Isaac and Darian hopped out of the back and respectfully assisted Jacob out of the wagon.

Best friends, Isaac and Darian walked ahead of the others. "Do you remember the first time we met?" Isaac asked.

"Yes, it was at the farm and you showed me all the fields, the river and the woods," Darian reminisced.

"Remember how scared you were of the beavers? America has the biggest rats in the world!" Isaac imitated.

Darian retaliated. "Remember the first day I went to school, and I had to beat up a bully, because you were too scared?"

The two young men laughed. "Did you ever think that one day you would be an American citizen and owner of your own business?"

"Partner," Darian corrected.

"All you ever wanted to do was to grow up, learn to shoot a gun, return to Ireland and kill the British."

"Well, I did grow up and learn to shoot. America is my home now. How about you? Did you ever think one day you would be married with children and living in your grandfather's house?"

"No." he said glumly.

The rest of the Miller men were ten steps behind. "Peter, is my sister still lamenting about how it is unfair that women cannot vote?" Eli asked.

"Rachel has a good point," Daniel defended his younger sister. "My wife is certainly capable of understanding the issues and voting wisely."

Eli scowled for he did not like his younger siblings to undermine his opinions. "I will agree that Rachel and Emily are unusually interested in politics. But most women are not qualified to …"

Two inebriated farmers staggered past them. "Some men are not qualified either," Peter nodded at the two. "Yet qualified or not, they still vote."

Jacob approved of his son-in-law for Peter and Rachel were a good match. Their arrival at the three, large, granite steps leading to the Town House ended their conversations. The Millers entered the crowded room.

"I have voted in every election since 1800," an elderly farmer boasted.

"Did you vote for Millard Fillmore?" a bystander asked.

"No. But if I had, I would deny it!" he shook his head.

Jacob and Eli laughed aloud. "Welcome!" Eli's brother-in-law and town selectman, Caleb Frye, greeted. "I see my favorite nephew skipped school today."

"Yes, sir." David surveyed the scene before him. There were merchants dressed in suits, blacksmiths with leather aprons and calloused hands, lumberjacks with wood chips in their wool coats, farmers with dirt on their leather boots, and attorneys in black coats and top hats. But there were no petticoats!

* * *

It was well after noon when the entire family converged at River View Farm. Kate and Julia spent hours preparing the meal and setting both tables. A pine trestle table dominated the kitchen and an elegant mahogany table graced the dining room. This one-hundred-year-old dining room set belonged to Aunt Grace. The men arrived first discussing crops, business and the price of lumber. A few moments later Emily opened the back door holding Summer's hand, followed by Lydia carrying a fidgety Mahayla.

"Lydia, you look… you look beautiful," Isaac complimented his wife. Her auburn hair was neatly put up. She took off her old black cape to reveal a dark green wool dress which complemented her green eyes. She smiled shyly at her in-laws.

"How lovely, you and the girls were able to make it," Kate warmly greeted.

"Papa!" Mahayla ran to Isaac and jumped into his outstretched arms. Summer held onto the folds of her mother's dress and quietly said, "Hi, Nana. Auntie made me bekfist. You make me lunch?"

"I certainly did! I made lunch for you and Mama, and Papa and Mahayla and Grandpa and…"

"And evy buddy!" Summer clapped her hands.

The kitchen door flew open. "I can only stay a short while. Peter needs me in the store and the boys will be home from school in a few hours," Rachel breathlessly entered and hung up her cloak. "What can I do to help?"

The ladies brought the food to the tables as the men and children took their seats. As platters of food were passed around, the front door opened and slammed. "Am I late for dinner?" David's best friend, Monroe asked.

Kate placed an extra plate on the kitchen table next to David.

"Monroe Quint, do you not have a family of your own?" Jacob teased.

"Oh yes sir. I have a fine family. But the food is so much better here!" The Millers laughed but Kate looked pleased.

Jacob stood in the doorway between the kitchen and the dining room. "My family came to America on the Mayflower to escape religious persecution and to worship God as they deemed fit. My own dear mother was a Quaker. In America the government does not tell you what church to attend, what to believe or what not to believe. In America everyone is equal under the law. We do not have royalty."

Rachel refrained from saying, "You mean men are equal. Women are not treated equal to men."

Daniel thought, "You mean white men are equal. Negroes and Indians are not treated equal to white men." Neither would ever contradict their father.

"In America any man has the opportunity to work where he pleases. He can own a farm or a store or a lumber mill. You are only limited by your ambitions. The government will not confiscate your property like the Marxists want to do in Europe. In America we vote for our leaders."

One look from her mother stopped Rachel from commenting.

"We are not ruled by kings or czars or sultans. We, American citizens, have rights. My grandfather and father were born British subjects. King George thought he had the right to claim the tallest and straightest pine tree anywhere in the colonies for masts in His Majesty's Royal Navy. My grandfather had one of the King's Pine right here in his woods. When he learned that the Declaration of Independence had been signed on July 4th back in 1776, he took his ax and chopped down that tree. My grandmother declared…"

"Some men declare their independence with a stroke of a pen. Others with a swing of an ax," David and Monroe recited in unison the oft told story.

"That is how the Liberty Table came to be," Monroe patted the long trestle table.

"And that was the day the Miller family became Americans," David concluded.

II

Snowstorms and Headlines

January 1861

Evans General Store was filled with customers buying needed supplies and patrons socializing with neighbors after a week of brutal cold and three snowstorms. As Rachel stood behind the counter, she spied Eli through the front window taking off his snowshoes.

"Eli, have you checked on Mama and Papa?" she anxiously greeted her brother as he entered.

"They are fine. Julia packed up clothing, food and schoolbooks and we headed over to the farm just as the first snow began to fall. We have been there all week. They are in good health and fine spirits now that they had a captive audience to listen to their stories," Eli laughed.

"Thank you. I know we can always depend on you, Eli. I was so worried about them."

"I know. That is why I stopped by. Pa also wanted me to buy some newspapers."

"I saved a few days' worth. We have not had many customers this week."

"Lincoln is an ugly son of a gun, ain't he?" Mr. Osgood pointed to the front page.

"I mean no disrespect to our new president, but I must agree with you," Eli replied.

"Our grandmother always said that man looks upon the outward appearance, while God looks at the heart," Rachel defended.

"Let us hope with a face like that he has a very good heart," Mr. Osgood joked.

"Do you think he will free the slaves?" Mr. Weston asked.

"The Constitution does not give a president the power to banish slavery where it already exists. A president can only stop it from spreading to the western territories.[1] At least that is what my grandfather told me," Eli replied.

"Not as if President Buchanan would take a stand against slavery," Rachel complained bitterly about the sitting president.

"President Buchanan is trying to hold this country together. That is the problem with you Millers and all abolitionists, you are unwilling to compromise!" another shopper declared.

"Shall we compromise with evil? Shall we compromise with tyranny? Did our Founding Fathers compromise with the British?" Rachel demanded.

"That is exactly what I mean. You think only you are right and everyone else is wrong!"

"The Founding Fathers wrote the Constitution and the Constitution allows slavery," someone else argued.

"Well nine out of the first twelve presidents owned slaves. For the past seventy-five years the federal government has been controlled by Southern slave supporters.[2] Personally, I welcome a self-made man like Abraham Lincoln. He is more like us than any of those slave-owning dandies!" Peter joined the debate.

"Hey, it is snowing again," someone observed.

"Thank you for the newspapers. Do not worry. I will take care of everything on the farm. I should head back," Eli explained as several customers who were listening to the discussion approached the counter with their purchases.

* * *

"Will it ever stop snowing?" Lydia muttered staring out the window.

"It is winter in Maine. It snows," Isaac shrugged. "What do you expect?"

"It did not snow like this last winter. We have not left the house in weeks," she complained.

"Mama, I am cold," Summer whimpered.

"This drafty old house is just too big to heat!" Lydia shivered.

"I can fix that," he winked at his daughters as he began moving all the dining room chairs into the front parlor.

"What on earth on you doing!" Lydia demanded.

"I am making the house smaller. You will see." He closed the door to the front parlor. "Now help me move the table against the wall."

"What on earth!"

"I will be back down in a few minutes." He spent the next half hour running up and down the back staircase carrying two corn husk-filled mattresses and every blanket and quilt he could find upstairs. He placed the girls' mattress under the table and draped a quilt over the table forming a tent. Then he placed their mattress on top of the table.

He closed off the front parlor, the entry and hallway and filled the kitchen's cookstove and dining room's woodstove with the well-seasoned hardwood.

The girls disappeared under the table and Summer poked her head out. "Like a house!"

"It can be a house or," he lifted the front quilt up onto bed above, "it can be a covered wagon. Shall we take a trip out west?" The girls squealed with delight as Isaac placed two kitchen chairs in front of the table.

"Where horse?" Mahayla asked.

"Make believe!" Summer admonished.

"Come, Mama," the girls invited.

Lydia silently stared out the window at the blowing snow.

"Mama is staying at the cabin to cook supper while we go shoot some buffalo," Isaac explained.

"Buffo?" Mahayla asked.

"Big, wild cows."

"We go shoot the buffos!"

* * *

The wind rattled the windows as Daniel, Darian and Emily huddled by the wood stove, each engrossed in their own projects.

"Emily, how many dresses do you plan to sew for the girls?" Daniel looked at the pile of clothing neatly folded on the table.

"These are not for Summer and Mahayla" she explained. "Pastor mentioned a few families who are in need. I am thankful to have a project to occupy the hours."

"I have completed all my bookkeeping. I have not been this organized since we built the mill. I dread the thought of shoveling," Daniel confessed as he stared at the snow drifts.

"Shoveling does sound like a healthy diversion right now. I have already read *Uncle Tom's Cabin* twice. I thought the British treated us Irish like slaves. Now I understand why some slaves are willing to risk their lives to escape to Canada," Darian commented.

"I could read *Oliver Twist* out loud," Emily offered. "I am a little tired of sewing."

Darian groaned. "Not again. What about the new novel Dickens wrote?"

"I left it at the farm for Ma to read," Daniel confessed. "If I had known we would be shut in for the month of January, perhaps I would not have been so generous."

"Fryeburg needs a library," Emily suggested.

* * *

"David, did I tell you about the time my father and I built a birch bark canoe?" Jacob asked.

"Yes, sir. Several times. It has always been my favorite story," he politely responded.

The family had closed off the upstairs, the front parlor and the dining room. The five of them sat around the Liberty Table. Eli was repairing a harness. Julia was chopping carrots and potatoes to make soup and David was studying Latin. Kate claimed the far end of the table where she was making salves.

"I think I will go feed the livestock," Jacob rose from the table.

Eli was tempted to remind his father that he had fed them only three hours ago. His concern increased as the hay in the hayloft decreased. Would they have enough hay to last until spring? "Good suggestion, Pa. I could stretch my legs and I am certain that the animals would benefit from the extra food in this cold."

"Bundle up, dear," Kate reminded her husband.

"What would I do without you?" he smiled at his wife.

"When you return, we will have tea and I will read another chapter of *A Tale of Two Cities*," Julia offered.

David stood up to leave as well. "Davy, did I tell you about the time my father and I planted the lilac bushes in front of his house?"

"Yes, sir. I think of that story every spring when I walk by them." David sighed. It was going to be a long winter.

* * *

"I am getting old," Daniel panted as he entered the kitchen.

"You two have been out shoveling for hours. Let Darian finish the path to the stable," Emily suggested.

"The sun is out. We thought we would hitch up the sleigh and take a visit to town."

"We could stop in the store to see Rachel and buy some thread. Then we could visit your parents," she excitedly suggested.

"And get *The Tale of Two Cities* back before it snows again." Daniel added

"Only if they are done reading it, of course."

* * *

Rachel did not notice the three of them enter.

"I say good riddance to them! Who needs them?" one man shouted.

"It is not a question of do we need them," Peter calmly responded. "It is a question of is it legal."

"Why not? If a state joined the union, is it not free to leave it?" someone else suggested.

"States cannot enter or leave the Union at will."

"What is President Buchanan doing about it?"

"What does he ever do about anything? Nothing. Nothing at all."

"He is leaving the mess for the new president to handle in March."

"Rachel, what is happening?" Daniel approached his sister.

"Oh, Danny, how are you? I haven't seen you since…"

"Election Day," Emily answered.

"I have saved some newspapers for you. Five states have seceded from the Union so far."

"So far?"

"Yes, there is talk that more southern states will follow South Carolina, Mississippi, Florida, Alabama and Georgia."

"But why?"

"South Carolina claimed that Lincoln is hostile to slavery. Remember that speech he gave on how a government cannot endure permanently half slave and half free?[3] I think they believed that was a threat to slavery, so the country would be wholly free."

"Do Pa and Eli know about this?"

"Everyone in Fryeburg knows about this!"

"This is merely the consequences of our country allowing slavery," Daniel lamented.

"The South has slaves, we do not," someone contradicted.

"I beg to differ. There is a slave named Limbo buried right behind the stone schoolhouse."

"Yes, that may be true, but that was a long time ago," a customer conceded.

Daniel continued, "When our grandparents were children during the War for Independence, they wore home spun wool or linen. If our great-grandparents could afford to purchase cotton fabric, it was manufactured in Britain from long staple cotton from India."

"Why would the British import cotton from India when it grew in the southern colonies?" another customer was drawn into the conversation.

"Because it is much quicker to pick the seeds out of long staple cotton grown in India. It would take a slave ten hours to pick out the seeds from one pound of cotton grown down South. After Eli Whitney invented the cotton gin back in 1799, that same slave can pick the seeds from fifty pounds of cotton in ten hours," Daniel explained.[4]

"Oh, I understand. It now became profitable to grow cotton in the South. Bigger profits led to the expansion of acreage to planting cotton," the first customer began.

"Of course, and the more cotton you grow, the more slaves you need to plant, tend and pick the cotton," the second customer continued.

"But still, we New Englanders do not plant cotton."

"We do not have to, to be culpable," Daniel chided. "New England has textile mills everywhere employing thousands of New Englanders and recent immigrants alike. Where do they get the cotton to weave the miles of fabric? The South of course. Sadly, one way or another we have all been complicit in slavery by either making, selling or buying the cotton fabric."

Some nodded with approval. "His grandparents would be so proud."

Others scowled. "Will these Millers ever learn to mind their own business? Who needs their sermons and lectures?"

Rachel's cheeks burned with anger.

Daniel turned to his sister, "I am sorry, Rachel, but our grandparents discussed this with all of us before you left to work in the mills in Biddeford."

She silently turned away for there was nothing she could say.

* * *

The month of March brought above-freezing day time temperatures and below-freezing temperatures at night. Eli, Jacob and Isaac loaded the old sleigh with newly washed wooden buckets, spiels and snowshoes and headed to the sugar bush.

"Beautiful day. It is good to see the sun and to work outside," Isaac commented as he drilled a hole in the maple tree with his auger.

"I hope Washington City is having good weather for the Inauguration." Eli developed his interest in politics by spending hours with his grandfather.

"What is an inauguration?" Isaac asked.

Eli shook his head with disgust. Jacob intervened before an argument ensued. "An inauguration is the ceremony where the new president takes the oath of office and gives a speech."

"Who is the new president?" Isaac asked innocently.

"Do not let your sister hear you say that! Everybody knows Abraham Lincoln won the election last November. What is wrong with you?" Eli chastised his younger brother.

"Are we here to work or are we here to argue?" Jacob challenged his sons.

"I am not arguing. I am educating like Grandpa would do if he was here. Did you hear about the other inauguration a few weeks ago?"

"Lincoln had two inaugurals?"

"No, Jefferson Davis had the inauguration," Jacob explained patiently.

"Even I know that America cannot have two presidents at the same time."

"Several southern states seceded from the Union, formed their own nation called the Confederacy and chose Jefferson Davis to be president."

"When did the Confederacy hold the election?" Isaac asked.

Jacob and Eli looked at each other. "That is a good question. I do not remember reading about an election in the newspapers," Eli admitted.

"Well, if he was not elected, how did he become president?" Isaac challenged. "Presidents are elected in a democracy. Is he a dictator? How did he become president?"

"He was elected without opposition. It merely confirmed what the Confederate Congress already decided.[5] Eli explained.

"You sound just like Grandpa," Isaac declared. "But what is going to happen?"

"I wish I knew, son. I wish I knew."

Round the clock sap boiling and political debates abruptly halted by a snowstorm followed six days later by another storm. Fryeburg did not know that a much larger storm was brewing.

III

War!

"Jacob, are you not hungry?" Kate asked with concern. "Are you unwell?"

"I am getting old, Katie," he admitted.

"We are both getting old. But it is better than the alternative," she laughed. "Now eat your breakfast."

"What would I do without you," he affectionately patted his wife's arm. "Remember when we were children and I took you for a canoe ride down the Saco River? I knew then, one day I would marry you…" The knocking at the kitchen door startled them. "Who could that be at this hour?" Jacob opened the door. "Peter!"

Kate stood up. "Peter, is Rachel all right?"

"Yes, mam. Rachel and the boys are fine. I thought you would like to have a this," he handed Jacob a copy of the day's newspaper. "I must hurry back to the store. I suspect it will be a very busy day."

"My father predicted this would happen. I just never thought it would happen in my lifetime."

Eli and David were headed toward the farm. "The snow is melting fast. It looks like we lost a good six inches yesterday," David observed.

"Let us hope that it does not melt too fast or we do not receive too much rain this April for we will have floods."

"And mud! Is that Uncle Peter?" David pointed to the figure leaving the farm.

Eli quickened his pace for he feared a family calamity.

He burst into the kitchen where he found his parents reading the newspaper, "Pa, is everything all right? I saw Peter leave."

Jacob handed them the paper. Eli and David read the headlines in stunned silence.

Isaac arrived shortly. "I just passed Peter on my way over. What is going on?"

Eli handed him the newspaper.

"Isaac, saddle up the horse and get Danny," Jacob instructed.

* * *

He found both Daniel and Darian planing oak boards at the mill. "Pa would like you to come to the farm right away," he announced breathlessly.

"Is Ma sick?" Daniel asked with concern. His mother took care of everyone. What would the family do if she was taken ill?

"No. Danny, we are at war!"

* * *

Daniel, accompanied by Darian and Emily, found his parents and Eli seated at the Liberty Table in a somber discussion.

"How did this happen?" Daniel asked before taking off his coat. Kate poured three cups of tea and placed a plate of buttered biscuits on the table.

"The South attacked Fort Sumter," Eli answered.

"I never heard of Fort Sumter. Where is it?"

"It is a fortress in the harbor of Charleston, South Carolina?"[1]

"That makes no sense. Why would the Confederacy attack a fort in South Carolina?"

"The fort belongs to the federal government, not the Confederacy. They were running out of supplies and asked for help," Eli explained. "President Lincoln had a choice. If he did nothing, that would have satisfied the South and avoided a conflict."

"It would avoid a conflict this week. But there would be another conflict next week. President Buchanan appeased the South and what did that get us? Losing Fort Sumter would be like losing the Union,"[2] Darian interjected.

"That is exactly right. President Lincoln pledged to hold, occupy and possess U.S. property. If he went against his word, he would alienate the Republicans who voted for him, divide the North and give recognition to the Confederacy,"[3] Eli continued.

"I do not know what Jefferson Davis is thinking. The South cannot possibly win," Jacob shook his head.

"It will be a short war. How can the South win?" Darian asked.

"We have ninety percent of the factories, steam engines, most of the trains. Our factories can make the guns and munitions and uniforms,"[4] Eli continued.

"Two thirds of the population live in the North. All the big cities, except New Orleans, are in the North. Most of the new immigrants, like the Irish, moved into the Northern cities because that is where all the jobs are,"[5] Darian continued. "You cannot win a war by planting cotton and drinking mint julip."

"You are both wrong," Daniel argued. "You are putting your trust in the wrong things. He quoted Psalm 20:7, "Some trust in chariots and some in horses; but we will remember the name of the Lord our God."

Eli shook his head. "War is about politics and economics, not religion."

"We live in a broken world ever since sin entered in the Garden of Eden. There have always been wars. This is not about the North and South." Daniel quoted Ephesians 6:12, "For we wrestle not against flesh and blood, but against principalities, against powers, against the rulers of the darkness of this world, against spiritual wickedness in high places."

Eli said nothing.

"You sound just like your grandmother," Jacob approved.

"Do you think that she would approve of this war?" Daniel challenged.

"Nana was a Quaker and Quakers are pacifists. Most of them did not fight in the Revolutionary War. If Nana had her way, we would still be British subjects," Eli argued.

"Let us pray for a short war," Emily suggested hopefully.

"Well, we may be at war, but I have livestock to feed and David, you need to leave for school. I am sure Maine is in no danger of an impending invasion," Eli observed dryly.

"We must return to the mill," Daniel stood up to leave.

"Danny, may I have a word with you?" Jacob stood up as well. "Eli, I will meet you in the barn shortly."

"We will wait for you in the sleigh," Emily suggested as Daniel followed his father to the front parlor.

"Take a seat," Jacob pointed to the old, faded settee as he took five leather bound journals from Aunt Grace's oak writing desk. "Do you remember these?" he handed his son the journals.

"Yes, I do. After Uncle Micah died, Aunt Grace wrote a history of Fryeburg. I should say her version of the history of Fryeburg. I miss her as much as a I miss Grandpa and Nana. But I do not understand."

"I want you to have them."

"I am honored, Pa. But the fifth one is blank."

"That one is for you to continue the story. I want you to write about this family and the war. Someday my descendants will read about this war, like you and I have read about Aunt Grace's version of the War for Independence."

"Pa, why me? Eli is the one interested in politics."

"You said yourself that this war is not about politics but something much darker. That is what you must write."

* * *

Rachel followed the unfolding events as she read the daily newspapers. Maine Governor Israel Washburn Jr. issued a call for ten regiments of volunteer infantry and three regiments of militia to be armed by the state.[6]

The rest of the Millers did not hear of it. Daniel and Darian were working around the clock. Now that the ice was out on the Saco River, the lumber mill hummed with activity. River View Farm was daily welcoming new arrivals, calves, foals and lambs. The snow was melting rapidly. Tools needed to be sharpened, livestock fed, cows milked, and butter churned. Fiddleheads and dandelions were the first to poke through the sodden ground.

Kate invited Isaac's and Eli's families to supper serving them fresh fiddleheads and dandelion greens dripping in butter and the last of a smoked ham.

"Ma, thank you for this delicious meal. I thought spring would never come," Isaac sighed with satisfaction.

"Lydia, you have plenty of fiddleheads and dandelions in your yard. Perhaps tomorrow I may take the girls outdoors to pick some. The fresh air will do them good," Kate suggested.

Mahayla clapped her hands in delight. "Nana! Nana!"

Summer looked dubious. "Too muddy." She had heard her mother repeat that phrase when Mahayla begged to go outside to play.

"Yes, it is muddy. That is why we will wear our old dresses. That is why I have a scrub board and a supply of lye soap," she smiled. "I raised three boys. I am not afraid of a little mud. Then I will teach your mama to make dandelion fritters."

"Thank you, Ma. I think all three of my girls will enjoy the excursion," Isaac accepted the invitation.

The next day, April 4, while they were picking dandelions, the state of Virginia seceded from the Union. The city of Richmond, located one hundred miles from Washington, became the new capital of the Confederacy.[1]

Lydia and two exuberant, rosy cheeked girls entered Kate's kitchen with baskets of freshly picked dandelions.

"First we pick the yellow flowers from the rest of the plant. Remove these little green leaves underneath because they are bitter," Kate instructed her granddaughters.

"Now mix 1/3 cup of flour and
1/3 cup corn meal,
a teaspoon of baking powder
a little honey
2 teaspoons of cinnamon, cloves, cardamom

Good stirring, Mahayla. Now, Summer, 1/3 cup of milk and crack the egg. Do not fret. We can pick out the eggshell. Practice makes perfect. Now stir it up.

This is a grownup job," she added lard to the hot fry pan.

Lydia dipped the flowers into the batter and Kate fried them in the pan.[8]

"What smells so good?" Jacob asked as he entered the kitchen followed by Eli and Isaac.

"We are cooking, Grandpa!" Summer explained.

"Licious!" Mahayla said with her mouth full.

The family was oblivious to the events transpiring in Washington City. The 6th Massachusetts Regiment arriving in Baltimore, Maryland on their way to Washington was attacked by a mob of Southern sympathizers. The soldiers fired to defend themselves. When the fighting was over, four soldiers and twelve citizens were killed.[9] When the Regiment finally arrived at the Capital, Clara Barton, a Massachusetts native working and living in Washington, noted their lack of necessities and began collecting food and supplies.

Secessionists destroyed railroad bridges and telegraph wires isolating Washington. Confederate campsites could be seen by the residents of the nation's Capital.[10]

On Sunday, July 21 the entire Miller family worshipped at the Congregational Church. Daniel's Rachel's and Isaac's families had Sunday dinner at their parents' home. Enjoying the food and fellowship they were unaware that the first major battle in the Civil War was underway in Virginia.

* * *

Thaddeus Pierce, journalist for the New York Post, walked the dusty streets of the nation's capital with distain. He had spent the past decade traveling throughout Europe visiting London, Paris and Vienna. "Of all the detestable places Washington is first. Crowds, heat, bad quarters, bad fare, bad smells and mosquitoes![11] Even the capitol building is unfinished."

Washington's elite were packing picnic lunches, purchasing battle maps and spy glasses in preparation for a six-hour carriage ride to the anticipated battlefield.[12] Thaddeus shook his head in disbelief. He had spent two years covering the Crimean War where he had witnessed first-hand the horrors of warfare. As the Union soldiers were marching off to battle, the civilians were riding to a Sunday afternoon frolic. He filled his flask with refreshment, hopped a ride with a reporter from the New York Times and join the caravan of sightseers headed for Manassas, Virginia.

Over sixty thousand troops converged at a river named Bull Run. During the morning Confederate troops had retreated; by noon many had taken flight over Henry House Hill disorganized and discouraged. When Confederate reinforcements arrived, the fighting continued into the early afternoon. By four o'clock the Confederates counterattacked and chased the retreating Union troops with cannon fire.[13]

With the last sip from his flask, Thaddeus joined the chaos of fleeing civilians, Union troops, ambulances and supply trains racing back to Washington. The Confederates won the first battle of the Civil War.[14] Thaddeus realized that he would not be returning to Europe any time soon. This promised to be a long, bloody war.

IV

Enlistment

The maple leaves by the lumber mill displayed the first signs of yellow this September morning. "Did Darian tell you where he was going?" Emily asked her husband as she washed the breakfast dishes.

"He did not, and I did not ask. He has worked six days a week for over seven years, and I figure he deserves a day off. Emily, he is not a child. He does not need our permission to go somewhere," Daniel reminded.

"Of course. You are right." She began drying the cups and saucers. "Do you think he has met a girl? A nice Irish girl?"

Daniel laughed. "You may ask him when he returns this evening."

It was well after dark when Darian arrived home. "Emily, you need not wait up for me," he protested, yet looked genuinely pleased to see that she had. "I am sorry that I am late. I stopped by Isaac's house to tell him the good news."

Daniel entered the kitchen. "Good news?"

"Yes, I went to New Hampshire where I qualified to become a member of the 1st United States Sharpshooter Regiment," Darian beamed with pride.

"A what?" Emily asked as she sat down at the kitchen table.

"You know the war is not going well," Darian began.

"I know that. I had hoped the war would have ended by now," Daniel agreed.

"You know that I am the best marksman in Fryeburg, possibly all of Oxford County. There is a man from New York named Hiram Berdan who is holding shooting contests. He is recruiting the best marksmen for two sharpshooting regiments. To qualify I had to stand upright and only using the iron sights of my rifle, I put ten consecutive shots in a target ten inches in diameter one hundred yards away. Not eight out of ten or nine out of ten, but all ten and I did it!"[1]

"You mean you are going off to fight in the war?" she failed to conceal the panic in her voice.

"Emily, please do not worry about me. I am a great shot."

"There is a big difference between hunting and fighting. The deer do not shoot back!"

"Darian, have you thought about the ramifications of this decision? Hunting to feed your family is one thing, but to take a life of another human being, another American, is different," Daniel began.

"Danny, I am not impulsive like Isaac. I have given this my deepest consideration. I am an American citizen now and I want to do more than just vote. Your grandfather always told me about the sacrifices that others before me made so we can enjoy the prosperity and freedom of America.

The Union forces are losing battles. I know that I may be forced to kill the enemy. By joining the sharpshooters, I can help the Union win the war and to win it quickly. I could be saving Confederate and Union lives in the long run by helping to end the war sooner."

"Darian, I am very proud of you. And I am sure that my grandfather would be proud of you as well."

"When do you leave?" Emily asked holding back tears.

"The end of the week for training. We are scheduled to join the fight in November."[2]

It was the middle of October and the foliage was ablaze with color. Two letters from Darian arrived at the general store.

"Peter, may I deliver this to Danny and Emily? It may be weeks before they stop by and I know Emily would be most grateful to hear a word from Darian," Rachel asked.

"You may as well deliver the second letter to Isaac while you are out. It is a glorious day for a ride. Who knows when it will snow?" Peter asked.

Emily opened the door. "Rachel, what a pleasant surprise. Do come in for a cup of tea."

Rachel held out the letter.

"Oh, thank you! Thank you!" she carefully opened the letter and sat down.

"I can make my own tea," Rachel offered.

October 5, 1861
Dear Emily and Danny,

My first train ride was an interesting experience. It was loud and smoky. I found observing the other passengers helped to pass the time. I did not spend much time in Portland, for there was only an hour between my arrival by stagecoach and departure by train. However, I did spend two days in Boston. I swear there are more Irish in Boston than there are in Dublin! Emily, I want you to know that I did meet one or two nice Irish girls that you would approve of. From there we took a boat to New York City. There are even more Irish in New York than in Boston.

The food is not bad. I spend most of my time drilling and marching. The weather is a little warmer down here in New York, although I hear it gets cold in the winter too. But I plan to be much further south when winter hits.

Just wanted to write you a few lines before I go to bed. Once we are south of the Mason/Dixon line I may be unable to continue our correspondence. Emily, I do not want you to worry. I will be fighting with the best trained Union soldiers.

Danny, please send my warmest regards to your parents and tell your mother I miss her cooking. When

I return after the war, we will build a big house where you will live with me, my nice Irish wife and twelve Irish children.

Fondly,
Darian

Emily reread the letter several times as Rachel finished her tea. "I have one more letter to deliver," she announced cheerfully.

"Rachel, thank you so much. I will show the letter to Danny. I dare say he misses Darian as much as I do."

* * *

"Potatoes, carrots, beets, rutabagas and apples. Every October is the same thing- harvesting potatoes, carrots, beets, rutabagas and apples. Next week will be chopping and stacking firewood. For once in my life I would like to eat food that I did not raise and warm myself by a fire which I did not chop the wood. Farming is so boring." He would never dare to utter those words aloud. His father, who was so proud of his farm, would consider this blasphemy. He heard a carriage approaching and saw Rachel waving to him.

"Where are you going?" Eli demanded as Isaac left the field.

"Pa, Rachel is here, and I think she has a letter. I am going to see," Isaac ignored his brother.

"You have a letter from Darian, and I thought you would be eager to read it," Rachel smiled as she stepped out of the carriage. "Is Mama in her herb garden?"

"Where else would she be?" Isaac sat down on the front steps and opened the letter.

Dear Isaac,

America is a very big country with very big cities. I am sure by war's end I will see even more of it. I hope I can go out West for a few battles and maybe even see some Indians.

They have issued us new guns, .54 caliber Sharps rifles. They weigh about ten pounds just like my old rifle, but they are a foot shorter.

Unlike the rest of the army where they stand shoulder to shoulder and fire volleys at one another, we will split into groups of two or three. With the shorter rifle, we can run through the woods, climb trees, lie down or kneel behind rocks.[3]

My Sharp can fire 10 rounds per minute. My old rifle can only shoot three. My Sharp has a cartridge of powder and bullet, but instead of a paper cartridge, I have a linen cartridge which is more combustible. It's a breechloader, loaded from the back instead of the front with a ramrod. Reloading is much faster and simpler requiring half as many steps. Those Rebs will not have a chance once we Sharpshooters enter the fight![4]

I will not be wearing a Union blue uniform. My uniform is green, so I can blend into the background. I even have black rubber buttons, so the sunlight's reflection on metal buttons will not reveal my location to the enemy.

Give the girls a hug from their Uncle Darian. Please write soon.

Your loyal friend,
Darian

* * *

It was early December when Rachel delivered another letter to Emily. "You are too kind to make a special trip out here," Emily gratefully accepted the letter. "Can you stay for tea?"

"I was planning on it." Emily was not listening.

Dear Emily and Danny,

Please thank everyone for their letters. It is such a comfort to hear from home. Please tell them I may not have time to write everyone, but I do think of them.
Emily, thank you for the package of socks and under drawers. But please stop. The men are accusing me of having a mistress, but I told them you are my American mother.

Emily put the letter down with tears in her eyes. "He called me his American mother!"
"Of course, you are. Everyone knows that."
"It is good to realize that he knows it too."
"Did he get his peppermints?"

Thank you, but I have more than enough and have even given a few pairs of socks away.
Please thank Rachel for the peppermints. They did not last long, for I shared them.
Christmas will soon be upon us. It will feel strange not to be celebrating it with the family at the farm. Please tell Mrs. Miller I will be thinking of her and her roasted potatoes with rosemary, roasted goose and smoked ham, mashed pumpkin and apple pies while I am eating salt pork and hard tack.

Merry Christmas,
Darian

"He sounds a little homesick, but he is doing well," Emily sighed with relief.

"Now, there is another matter I wish to discuss," Rachel put down her teacup. "As you know I make a considerable profit from the sale of fabrics and sewing notions. Since the war began, the Northern textile mills lost their supply of cotton. Some factories have shut down due to the lack of cotton, others have converted to producing weapons. Some mills have remained in business as they illegally import cotton from the South."

"Is that not treason?" Emily asked.

"No, it is business," Rachel calmly replied.

"Have you bought any of that fabric?"

"Not yet, and I hope I never have to. But I have a business to run and children to feed. The price of some fabrics is rising, and many women are struggling to make ends meet while their husbands have left for war. Many women simply take apart older dresses and remake them into newer styles.

You are an artist with a needle and thread. Could you sew two identical dresses? One will be unadorned and the second with a new collar, undersleeve, lace and trim. I am sure women will buy the fabrics and notions. I will pay you for your services."

"I will certainly have the time this winter."

"I was hoping you would say that. I have some fabric and a basket of trim in the wagon."

When Rachel returned, Emily marveled at the trim. "What plants produce such vibrant colors?"

"These ribbons and trims were dyed with a chemical dye made by a German company."

"This will be quite satisfying. I will have plenty of time this winter."

* * *

After Christmas Isaac entered the general store with Summer and Mahayla. "How are my two favorite girls?" Rachel warmly greeted. "Look at those rosy cheeks! Stand by the stove and warm up. Isaac, I have a letter for you and one for Emily and Danny."

"I can take the girls in Grandpa's sleigh and deliver it to them," He offered. "The girls could use a change of scenery." Isaac read his letter.

Dear Isaac,

This is for your eyes only and please do not mention this to Emily. I have been in two battles. I killed ten Rebels in the first one and nineteen in the second one. The first battle happened so fast I did not have time to be scared. I am well trained, and I simply did my job.
I lost two friends in the second battle. It is a terrible thing to see a man die a few inches from you. It is more terrible to see a man die, knowing you were the one who killed him.
I am not a praying man, but you are sometimes. Please pray for me when you are in church on Sunday. I have been thinking about all the things your grandparents told me when I was a boy.
Remember how upset your grandmother was when I got into a fight with the school bully? She said Christians should not fight. Yet your grandfather was proud of me for taking a stand and defending Davy and Monroe who were too little to defend themselves. Do you turn the other cheek, or do you fight? Every day I ask myself, who was right.
Give the girls a hug from Uncle Darian.

Your loyal friend,
Darian

Isaac swallowed the lump in his throat. "Come on girls, let us ask Mama if she would like to take a sleigh ride to visit Aunt Emily."

"Aunt Emmy," Summer clapped her hands.

The four of them arrived at the mill just after lunch. "What a surprise! Come in. Come in. I shall put the water on for tea," Emily invited.

"We brought you a letter," Lydia handed her the precious correspondence.

"Thank you. Lydia, you and the girls are always welcome to visit with or without a letter. First, I shall read and then I shall brew us some chamomile tea."

Dear Emily and Danny,

Please thank everyone for their Christmas wishes and gifts. Please tell Mrs. Miller how much I appreciate her teas and salves. The men teased me and said I could open my own apothecary. I think they are jealous.

Thank you for The Tale of Two Cities. I have long periods of time in my tent with not much to do. Emily, please do not worry about me for I have plenty of underdrawers and socks, teas to drink, a new book to read, a family to love and adequate food but not as good as home. All is well.

I am doing my best to end this war and come home soon. I need to write a letter to a nice Irish girl in Boston before I go to bed.

Fondly,
Darian

Emily looked up and smiled. "Please stay for supper."

* * *

By late summer of 1862 the war was going poorly. The Union's battle to take Richmond, Virginia failed miserably. To compensate for the causalities sustained in the campaign, the North called for 300,000 volunteers. The state of Maine responded with five regiments.[5]

David entered his grandmother's kitchen with a copy of the newspaper. His parents and grandparents were taking a brief morning respite. "Monroe and I are going to Portland to volunteer."

"I need you on the farm, son," Eli objected.

"Danny needed Darian at the mill as well and he is managing. The country needs me more than the farm does."

"Just because Monroe is enlisting does not mean that you have to," Julia added.

"You are wrong, Ma. I am not enlisting because of Monroe. He is enlisting because of me."

"Why do you wish to fight this war? For the adventure? For the $25.00 bounty?" Jacob calmly questioned.

"No, for my country. Remember when I was a little boy and your father asked me if I wanted to become President?"

"I am sure you will be a better President than Millard Filmore," Jacob repeated.

"I want to be President of the entire United States, not just half. We cannot allow slavery to keep expanding west. Where will this all end, if we do not put a stop to it? My decision is made. If I leave now, I will be back before dark. May I take the wagon?"

"My wagon is at your disposal," Jacob offered.

* * *

"It is awfully early. Where are you and Monroe headed?" Isaac stopped the wagon as he was leaving his back door.

"To Portland to enlist," David answered.

Isaac hopped in the back of the wagon. "I have not been to Portland in years. I am coming too."

"To Portland or to enlist?"

"I have not decided yet."

It was after dark when Isaac arrived home. "Where have you been?" Lydia angrily greeted him at the door. Eli told me you never showed up to the farm."

"Well, he better become accustomed to it, for I will not be around for long."

"What are you talking about?" she demanded.

"I have enlisted in the 17th Regiment of Maine and will be leaving at the end of the week."

"What! You are leaving me? You are leaving the girls? You are just like my father!"

"I am nothing like your father! Your father left you and your mother for his mistress in Conway. I am leaving to fight for my country. I am getting a $25.00 bounty for you and the girls. I will send you my monthly pay. It is only temporary. I will be coming back soon."

"You do not know that. This war could drag on for years. The girls will not know you when you return. What about me?"

"Lydia, you are never happy. I have given you one of the largest and finest homes in Fryeburg. It is furnished with the finest furniture. What more do you want from me?"

"Love," she snapped.

"I do love you. I gave up going to college and becoming a lawyer like my grandfather to marry you. I wanted to continue my grandfather's law firm when my cousin left the country. I wanted to show Eli that I could be somebody. When your mother killed – died unexpectedly, you had no one to take care of yourself. I was afraid you would become like your mother to support yourself or go to the poor house."

"How dare you!"

"I asked my parents to pay for your mother's cemetery plot and tombstone, so she would not be buried in a pauper's grave. When my aunt and uncle were killed the next week in the carriage accident, I inherited this house according to my grandfather's will. The first thing I did was marry you and provide you a home and a good family. And my grandfather's office remains locked."

"You Millers think you are better than everyone else."

"That is not fair. My family, especially my mother, has tried to welcome you into this family. All you do is reject them. The deed has been done. I am leaving."

"Who will take care of us?" she cried.

"My mother will teach you to cook. Emily will teach you to sew. Danny will see to it that the woodshed is filled for the winter. If you are lonely, you can invite someone to visit. You are a Miller now and it is time you conduct yourself like one. I expect my daughters to have a mother they can be proud of."

"How dare you!"

"I am leaving at the end of the week. I will talk to Emily and Danny about helping you out. It is your decision how you will handle my absence. For the girls' sake I hope you choose wisely."

Lydia was absent when the entire Miller family congregated on the main street to wave goodbye to Isaac, David, Monroe and the other Fryeburg men. Danny and Emily held Summer and Mahayla so the girls could wave goodbye to their father as the wagon left for Camp King in Cape Elizabeth.

The 17th Maine, consisting of one thousand men, ten companies with one hundred men each, trained for two and a half weeks before being called to Washington. From Camp King they marched to Portland where they took a train to Boston. It was the first train ride for the three young men. It was a great adventure as they continued to Providence, Rhode Island by train and to Jersey City, New Jersey by steam ship. Here they were visited by the American Bible Society and received a pocket New Testament. With Bibles in hand they boarded trains to Philadelphia, Baltimore and finally the nation's capital.[6]

From Washington City the men could hear the battle raging at nearby Antietam, Maryland. Isaac wondered out of the one thousand men, how many would make it home. How many would be killed on the battlefield? How many would die from camp diseases? How many would desert? Would he live to see his daughters grow up?

For Isaac Miller, the adventure was over. The war had begun.

V

The Home Front

Fryeburg, Maine September 1862

"It is not Sunday. Why are you all dressed up?" Mahayla asked her sister as she entered the kitchen.

"It is the first day of school. Aunt Emily made this dress for me," Summer explained.

"I am not going to school," Mahayla crossed her arms against her chest.

"There are books to read and new things to learn every day. I will be a teacher when I grow up."

"I have more important things to do than sit around all day inside a school when I could be in the garden working with Nana."

"Well Mahayla, you will not be attending school this year," Lydia reminded.

"I am never going to school," she stomped her foot.

"Mahayla Anne, that is most unladylike. We will have this discussion next year," her mother firmly stated.

Emily smiled at her young sister-in-law and said nothing. She was grateful that she and Daniel decided to move in with Lydia and the girls a few months ago. Her nieces were thriving with some structure and discipline. Lydia was becoming more comfortable in her role as a mother with the support of her in-laws.

There was a light rap on the kitchen door before Kate entered. "Summer, are you ready for the big day? You look lovely in your new dress."

"Thank you, Nana. But school is about learning and not about pretty dresses," Summer reminded.

Kate laughed. "You are correct, young lady."

"Nana, did you come to take me to the farm?" Mahayla asked hopefully.

"I came to join your mother and walk your sister to school."

"The school is right across the street. She can walk herself to school."

"The first day of school is an important milestone. Your grandmother and I will escort your sister. Stop being impertinent, or you will go to your room all morning."

"When I return, I will take you back to the farm with me," Kate promised as she left the house with Lydia and Summer. "I remember Isaac's first day of school. It seems like it was only yesterday when I walked him to this very school. As I recalled, he did not want to go. He wanted to stay home and help me with the garden."

"Mama, did you go to this school too when you were a little girl?"

"No. I lived in East Fryeburg and went to the school there."

Summer hesitated, clutching her slate and copy book. "Now you run along and play with those little girls. When the teacher comes out to ring the bell for the start of school, line up with the girls," Kate calmly explained.

"Mama, will you watch from our front door?"

"Yes, I will be just across the street. When the church clock strikes twelve, I will wait at the front door for you to come home for lunch," she promised before she and Kate returned to the Millers' front yard. The bell rang, the girls lined up and entered school before the boys.

Lydia and Kate entered through the rarely used front door.

"I made a pot of tea," Emily invited.

"Thank you, dear. After my tea, I think I will bring my little helper back to the farm with me. Today is a churning day."

"Nana, did you learn to make butter in school?"

"No, Mahayla. My grandmother taught me."

Mahayla gave her mother an "I told you so" look. Emily looked out the window to stop herself from laughing.

"Finally," Mahayla sighed as her grandmother put down her empty teacup.

"Finally," Kate laughed as she stood up to leave. "Everyone is invited over to supper tonight to celebrate Summer's first day of school."

"Do you mean I can spend the whole day with you? This day keeps getting better!"

"For both of us," Lydia thought with a smile as she watched her daughter and mother-in-law walk up the road toward the farm.

"I do believe this is the first time in five years I do not have a child with me," Lydia declared.

"I certainly admire you," Emily began for she hoped to have a day alone with her.

"Whatever for?" she asked suspiciously.

"Look how well your daughters are growing up even with Isaac being away for a year."

"It is because of you and Danny and not because of me."

"You have not had it easy. Your mother died, you got married, moved into this huge house and had a baby within a year. Then had another baby the next year. When Julia had her first child, her mother came over several times a week, did all her laundry, cooked meals. When Mother and Father Miller had Eli, Danny and Rachel, they lived in this house with his parents. His mother helped with the children as well as cooked most of the meals and helped with all the laundry. When Isaac was born eighteen years later, they were living at the farm with Aunt Grace and Uncle Micah. Aunt Grace and Hannah Miller practically raised him while she was busy on the farm.

Who did you have to help? I grew up with three brothers and three sisters. My mother and grandmother taught us girls to cook, sew and clean. I was never blessed with children, so I did not have to divide my attentions between children and domestic duties.

My mother gave me this book thirty years ago. It is a bit old fashion, but I want to pass it on to you," she handed a well-worn book.

"*The Frugal Housewife* by Lydia Childs. Well thank you. This is the first book I have ever owned. My mother never had money for extravagances like books. I will read it when the girls are asleep."

"It is a beautiful day. After we do the dishes, shall we take a walk to see Rachel at the general store? She can keep us abreast on the news and perhaps we have some letters waiting for us," Emily suggested.

After the dishes were washed, dried and put away and the kitchen was tidy, the ladies put on their bonnets. Emily grabbed her willow shopping basket.

The bell over the door announced their arrival. As Rachel was busy selling glass mason jars to several ladies, Emily led Lydia to the shelves with the fabric and sewing notions.

"Emily, I will not allow you to make the girls another dress."

"I have another idea. You know I have two trunks filled with scraps of fabrics. I am going to buy three needles, three thimbles and another pair of scissors. We are going to make some new bed quilts. Isaac's grandmother's quilts are at least fifty years old. It is time for new ones, and we may store those old treasures in a trunk."

"Do you really think you could teach me to sew?"

"Of course, I can. I taught Darian to sew before he left. The girls are old enough to begin to sew a few simple stitches. It will be a good winter project."

"Yes, the winters are dreadfully long," Lydia agreed.

"Not if you have projects to keep you busy."

"Is Summer at school today?" Rachel greeted.

"Yes, she is and Mahayla is spending the day with your mother," Lydia smiled.

"Then you have time to visit," Rachel invited. "I just read an article about an extraordinary woman named Clara Barton. She is a nurse."

"Yes, there are many dedicated women nursing our wounded soldiers in hospitals," Emily agreed.

"But Miss Barton is treating wounded soldiers right on the battlefields! She is the first woman to ever do so and at great risk to her life. Too many soldiers die on the battlefields waiting to be taken to a hospital. She is saving lives!"

"Let us pray that our men will never need her services," Emily tried to change the subject.

"I would like to buy a newspaper," Lydia stated.

"I have four or five newspapers left over from last week. They are in the back. Let me get them for you. Otherwise, they will become kindling."

"Do you think that is wise? The papers are filled with stories about the war," Emily warned. "Although I am certain they are exaggerated just to sell papers."

"That may be true. However, there are other stories to read as well."

"Here you are," Rachel handed Lydia the papers.

"Thank you. Emily and I are going to make some quilts," she proudly announced.

"Yes. I will be purchasing these items," Emily put the sewing notions on the counter.

Lydia scanned a newspaper. "My gracious! Do you know you can buy meat in a tin can?"

"Who would ever buy food in a dirty can?" Mrs. Osgood, who was standing in line, exclaimed with disgust.

"It would take a tinsmith several hours to make a can," Mrs. Weston added.

"The cans are made in a factory," Rachel explained.

"How is one supposed to open a tin can?" Mrs. Osgood challenged.

"There is a tool called a can opener," Rachel explained.

"I suppose these can openers are made in factories as well?" Mrs. Weston asked.

"Yes, they are," Rachel agreed.

"This is just a passing fad," Mrs. Osgood predicted.

* * *

"Uncle Eli, I am spending the entire day on the farm. My sister went to school, but I am not going to school," Mahayla announced as she entered the barn.

Her uncle nodded. "I remember when your Aunt Rachel was your age and would help your grandmother. But she was not interested in butter and gardens and staying on the farm. She wanted to have a job and make money."

She quietly pondered that thought. "Nana is calling me!" She ran to the house.

* * *

Emily and Lydia spread out pieces of fabric on the dining room table. "Look at all the different colors. How will we ever decide?" Lydia exclaimed.

"What are Mahayla's favorite colors?" Emily asked.

"Blue and green like the sky and the grass."

"We will make her quilt first. We will select all the blues and greens and some whites and yellows. For our first quilt, we will sew together squares. We will attempt some other patterns in the future. This way even the girls can sew a few squares."

As they inspected each remnant Lydia asked, "How did your mother get all her housework done while watching you and your brothers and sisters?"

"She had a schedule. Monday was laundry. Tuesday was ironing, Wednesday was mending, Thursday was baking, and Friday was cleaning. We children were expected to help. The boys brought in the firewood and buckets of water. When I was Mahayla's age, I gathered all the dirty clothes and help put away the clean clothes. My brothers started the fire and filled the wash and rinse tubs with water. My mother washed the clothes in the wash tub, my sister and I put them in the rinse tub. We thought that was great fun. My oldest sister wrung them and hung them on the clothesline. I was too small to reach.

My mother was very particular about ironing our church clothes and school clothes, but not our work clothes. As soon as we returned from school or church, we would change into our work clothes. Of course, we were isolated living in the woods near the river. Our work clothes sometimes needed mending, and they were never ironed.

My mother learned to cook on the hearth as a girl. She was not pleased when my father surprised her one day with a cook stove. She said she had to learn to cook all over again. We girls learned together how to control the temperature of the oven."

"How do you control the temperature?"

"Practice. Much practice. We ate many a piece of burnt bread, but my father knew better than to comment. Mostly my mother cooked soups and she would add more vegetables or scraps of meat to the pot every day. Every Saturday she baked beans and we would heat up the beans for Sunday dinner.

Now Isaac's mother is a much fancier cook. Because she had family to help watch the children, to do the laundry, sweep and tidy the house, she was free to work in her gardens, preserve food, make butter, cook and bake. I think Isaac's grandmother did all the mending.

Next year both girls will be in school and you will have quiet, uninterrupted hours for housework.

"Next year the war will be over," Lydia predicted.

"I pray so."

* * *

"Nana, this is boring. I have been churning all day!"

"I have been churning for an hour and you have been at it for ten minutes," Kate corrected.

"Are we done now?"

"What did we hear when we began?"

"Splashing because the churn was filled with cream."

"Then what did we hear?"

"Nothing because it turned into thick whipped cream."

"Now listen while you churn."

"I hear a little bit of splashing."

"What does that mean?"

"The butter is separating from the butter milk. I am making butter!"

"Ten more minutes without complaining and we will have butter."

Ten minutes felt like an eternity. "Nana, listen. I think it is time to take the cover off and look."

"I think you are right."

"Look! I see butter!"

"What do we do first?"

"Drain the buttermilk. I will get your milk pitcher." She intently watched her grandmother pour the buttermilk as she held back the chunks of butter with a wooden paddle. Kate used the paddle to scrape the butter out of the churn and into a large bowl.

"Are we done now?" Mahayla asked impatiently.

"No. I need to wash any drops of buttermilk off the butter. Please hand me the tin pitcher of water." She poured some water over the butter, swirled it around with a wooden spoon and poured the cloudy water into a nearby tin basin. She repeated this step two more times, until the water was perfectly clear.

"Are we done now?"

"No, I need to press any excess water out and then pack them in my wooden molds."

"Why?"

"Because I want each brick of butter to be a pound and people will recognize my flower design and know that I was the one who made the butter."

"Why?"

"Because everyone knows I make the best butter in Fryeburg and I want to sell them at Aunt Rachel's store."

"Why?"

"I will either trade my butter for flour and baking powder or get paid in cash."

"Why?"

"It is very important for a woman to know how to make her own money."

Mahayla quietly pondered that thought as she helped spoon the soft butter into the wooden molds.

"Now we are done," Kate declared with satisfaction. "Please take this basket to the cellar and fill it with apples from the barrel. Those cellar stairs are a strain on my knees. We are going to bake two apple pies for tonight's supper."

* * *

Lydia opened the front door and greeted, "Dinner is ready. Tell me about your morning."

"Some of the boys are not well behaved and had to sit in the corner wearing a dunce cap.

I already know everything in the Primer of the McGuffey's Readers and the teacher had me sit with some older girls and share Book I. The teacher told me that I had very neat printing and said I must have practiced at home. I told her Aunt Emily and I practiced my letters and numbers. All the girls brought jump ropes. Can I bring a jump rope to school tomorrow?"

"Of course, you can," Emily agreed.

"Mama, I can walk back to school by myself. I will look both ways for horses and wagons before I cross the street."

After a quick dinner, Summer skipped out the front door to enjoy a few minutes of recess before the afternoon session.

"Emily, I do not have a jump rope to give her."

"Of course, you do. This afternoon we will make the clothesline a little bit shorter," Emily laughed.

* * *

The family gathered around the Liberty Table in the kitchen. "I helped peel the apples and make the butter," Mahayla announced.

"Did you have a good first day of school?" Jacob asked.

"Yes, Grandpa. I like it very much." Summer replied.

"I remember David's first day of school. I walked with him, even though his two older sisters were with him," Julia reminisced.

"Let us pray that David, Darian and Isaac will soon be sitting at this table eating with us," Daniel tried to sound cheerful.

"Let us not forget Monroe," Kate added.

Jacob laughed. "No one could forget Monroe."

* * *

Both girls were exhausted and promptly went to bed without the usual fuss. Lydia lit the lamp in the front parlor, sat down on the settee and opened her book.

The true economy of housekeeping is simply the art of gathering up all the fragments, so that nothing be lost. I mean fragments of time, as well as materials. Nothing should be thrown away so long as it is possible to make any use of it, however trifling that use may be.[1]

Lydia resolved that every evening she would spend at least a half an hour reading the *Frugal Housewife* and the newspaper. She would become as knowledgeable as Rachel about the war and world events. Tomorrow she would ask Emily for her first cooking lesson. She would learn how to make soups and suppers from whatever fruits, vegetables and herbs her mother-in-law gave her. She would invite guests over to dinner and serve meals in the dining room on Hannah Miller's best china.

She would show Mahayla the blue and green fabrics for her quilt and begin to cut squares. She was determined to learn to sew. Each bed would have a new quilt. She and her daughters would be the best dressed women in Fryeburg. Above all, Lydia would prove that she is not her mother!

VI

The Schaeffer Family

Gettysburg, July 1, 1863

Mrs. Carolyn Schaffer was a petite but formidable woman. She was thrilled when she and her husband, Carl, moved to Gettysburg five years ago, where he established a busy law practice near the Adams County Court House. Gettysburg, with a population of 2400, offered all the amenities she desired. There were several churches, a variety of merchants and shops, newspapers, a college and a seminary.[1] She immediately became involved in the ladies' ministries at St. James Lutheran church and her four children were good students at the public school. Mrs. Schaffer was a charming hostess often entertaining her husband's clients of bankers, editors and college professors.

After Carl's untimely death two years ago, she sold the law firm and bought a new sewing machine. She converted the front sitting room in her two-story brick house located further south on Baltimore Street into her shop where she custom made clothing for the well-heeled men and women of Gettysburg.

Three months ago, she warmly welcomed Martha, a young, pregnant neighbor whose husband had enlisted in the army. The children were thrilled two weeks ago when they found a beautiful baby girl upon their arrival home from school. The Schaffer family lavished much love and attention on Baby Anna.

Mrs. Schaeffer was much too busy to listen to the gossip of an impending invasion. When the Rebels marched into town on June 26th, she closed her shutters, locked her doors and continued her sewing. When the invaders left the next day, she unlocked her doors, opened the shutters and continued sewing. On June 30th, she escorted the children, Martha and Baby Anna outside to clap and cheer when the first of the Union troops arrived.[2] The town made a collective sigh of relief for they believed they were now safe. They were wrong.

This morning the family awakened to the sounds of battle. As Rebel shells began to explode near and in town, citizens needed to quickly decide to leave their homes for safety or remain in their cellars for the duration of the fighting. Baltimore Street was a scene of chaos and confusion where civilians tried to avoid the marching soldiers and passing artillery. Anxious mothers scolded, terrified children cried, and the elderly did their best to hurry to safety. Mrs. Schaeffer moved her sewing machine, fabrics and family into the relative safety of the basement. There was no time to run outside to close the shutters for the battle had begun.

* * *

David Miller slowly opened his eyes. Heat, thirst, the pounding of his head and the ringing of his ears assailed him. He felt the ground tremble beneath his body with each cannon shot. He closed his eyes as the sights and sounds of the raging battle drifted away. Thirty minutes later he was awakened by a nearby exploding shell and a bloody torso landing on his body. He wiped the gore off his face with the back of his hand.

"Monroe! Monroe!" he screamed. "Isaac! Isaac!" No one heard. He painfully rolled over on his side, knocking off the torso. He propped himself up on one elbow and slowly drew himself up on his hands and knees before collapsing. With a racing heart and shaking hands he managed to pull himself on his hands and knees a second time. He slowly stood on trembling legs and staggered away unnoticed in the deafening chaos.

He knew not the day nor the hour as he frantically searched for Monroe and Isaac. Several times he tripped over broken bodies which sent him sprawling to the ground. Twice he remained motionless in the grass hoping that death would find him. Each time he struggled to his feet and continued his journey into confusion.

He spied several blue coats in a distant yard behind a two-story brick house. He plodded onward and collapsed in the shade of a tree.

He remembered that blue coats were good. He could find Monroe and Isaac if he stayed with the blue coats. You shoot the gray coats. He closed his eyes and then reopened them to confirm these soldiers indeed wore blue coats.

"Please have some water," a woman's voice interrupted his haze of confusion. She filled his canteen with water from her pail. He greedily gulped it down.

"Are you hungry? Would you like some bread?" He nodded.

"Where am I? What time is it?"

"Baltimore Street. Midafternoon. I will return with some bread and more water."

David looked around in a daze. The yard was filled with retreating Yankee troops. "Here you go," Mrs. Schaeffer returned with two slices of bread.

"Are we in Virginia?"

"No. We are in Pennsylvania. You need to get some rest." Her kind and compassionate voice reminded him of his mother.

"You need to get inside. It is not safe for you out here," he warned. An infant's wail pierced the air. "I hear a baby!"

"That is my neighbor's baby. Poor little thing!"

Gun shots rang out from across the street. "I best return to the kitchen and bake more bread." As she reentered her house, she admonished her ten-year-old son, "Oliver, away from the windows and return to the cellar."

"It is more exciting up here," he argued.

Martha was sitting in a chair trying to console her screaming infant.

"Bad time to be born," Oliver muttered.

Martha burst into tears for the strain and exhaustion of the past few weeks overwhelmed her.

"There is never a bad time to be born," his mother contradicted. "A new life born in the midst of death, innocence born into a world of hatred, hope of a better future during our present difficulties. Now everyone, please down to the basement while I bake more bread."

Early the next morning Thursday, July 2 David confiscated a rifle from a dead soldier in the yard. There were many dead soldiers dressed in blue. He worried if that was stealing, but he needed a gun to protect the family of women and children who lived in the brick house. Concerned that the kind lady could be shot if she stepped outdoors to feed the troops, he felt it was his duty to protect his benefactress. He counted at least 150 bullet holes marring the outside of the house as he awaited her arrival.

The kitchen door opened, and the kind lady stepped out with two willow baskets filled slices of bread. She smiled kindly at David and gave him the first slice before walking through her yard distributing bread to the famished soldiers. She did not notice her eight-year-old daughter quietly slip out the door to follow her. Gunfire once again erupted from across the street. David grabbed the terrified child, threw her on the ground, shielding her with his body.

"Alice!" the kind lady screamed as she came running to the crying child.

"She is not hurt, mam," David reassured her. "You and your family need to stay inside. Let the soldiers distribute the bread and water."

She sadly shook her head. "That was the last of the bread. There is no more flour."

David escorted mother and daughter back to the kitchen. "Thank you for your protection. I will never forget your bravery."

The next morning, July 3rd rumors spread that a twenty-year-old woman was shot and killed while baking bread three houses up the street.³ David was thankful that the kind lady and her family were safe in the cellar but concerned they had no food left.

He decided to leave the yard in search of food to give to the family. That was the last time he was seen by the blue coats. David Miller disappeared.

VII

The Gunther Family

July 1, 1863 Gettysburg, Pennsylvania

For the past few weeks, Joseph and Emma Gunther had heard the rumors of an impending invasion. When other merchants had shipped their goods out of town by train to protect their inventory,[1] Joseph decided to keep Gunther's Mercantile on West Middle Street open. His customers depended upon him for more than hardware, sewing notions, tools, pots, pans and the daily newspaper. It was a place for friends and neighbors to congregate, where bereaved parents and widows came to purchase black fabric and children ran in after school to buy penny candy. Several customers stopped in regularly to talk about the weather, crops, family news and politics. When one frail gentleman failed to appear for two days, Emma went to his home where she found him lying on the floor where he had fallen.

This morning Joseph and Emma heard gunfire in the distance coming from Seminary Ridge.[2] Soon the ground shook with the roar of cannons. Merchandise began to rattle on the shelves, some crashed to the floor. Joseph turned to his wife, "Quickly, take Henry to my brother's farm. You will be safer there."

"I am not leaving without you!" Emma protested.

"I must stay here and guard the store. Who else will check on our neighbors?"

Twelve-year-old Henry came running into the kitchen. "Papa! What is happening?"

"Some fighting has broken out. Now take your mother to Uncle John's farm. You will be safer a few miles out of town. I will store as much inventory that I can in the cellar. If the fighting gets too close, I will seek shelter in the cellar as well. I expect you to be brave and leave!" he commanded.

Henry obediently took his mother's arm and escorted her out the door. They were not the only residents leaving the area. Baltimore Street quickly filled with panicked people fleeing danger.

When they finally reached Taneytown Road, Emma feared they made a mistake as they passed their first ambulance. Henry silently squeezed his mother's arm as they watched a line of Union soldiers, wagons and artillery pass them. They quickened their steps when a Union soldier shouted, "Turn back. It is not safe!"

"Our destination is just over the hill," Emma pointed. There was no turning back now!

They were greatly relieved when they spotted the familiar white farmhouse neatly framed by a picket fence with a large barn by a spring.

Seventeen-year-old Maggie Gunther looked out the dining room window to watch the procession of soldiers marching by when she spotted her aunt and cousin hurrying toward the house. "Pa, Aunt Emma is coming!"

John Gunther ran outside, safely escorted the family to his home, slammed and locked the door."

* * *

Joseph was panting from the exertions of running up and down the cellar steps. He had moved the most valuable of his inventory, bags of flour and sugar, tins of meat, tea and coffee beans, tools and nails. After the battle his customers would need to eat and rebuild damage to their homes.

A frightened elderly couple pounded on the front door. "May we seek the comfort of your family's company for the duration of the battle?"

"I sent my family to my brother's farm. But please come in and make yourselves comfortable upstairs in our apartment. If the fighting comes too close, I will escort you to the cellar."

Two Union soldiers burst open the unlocked door. One was wounded and unarmed. "The Rebels are just down the street and will be here soon!"

"Take Mr. and Mrs. Peterson upstairs and hide in a bedroom closet. Mrs. Peterson please make some tea and sit in the kitchen."

"Why not the cellar?" one soldier argued.

"That is the first place they will look. Now hurry!" Joseph locked the door.

Ten minutes later gunfire erupted shattering his front windows. Rebel soldiers kicked down the front door demanding, "Where are they?"

"I sent my family to my brother's farm on the outskirts of town three hours ago."

"We saw two soldiers run in here! Now, where are they!" he pointed a rifle at Joseph's head.

"Yes, they did run in here. I helped them escape through the back door into the alley," Joseph explained.

"He's lying! Check the cellar!"

Three soldiers ran down the stairs while two opened the back door to search the alley.

"I see your wagon, but where is your horse?"

"My horse? They stole my horse?" Joseph feigned indignation. As soon as his family left, he rode his horse to the woods, left him there with a sack of oats and ran home.

"There is no one in the basement but we discovered these," one private held up a sack of flour.

"Very good." As a line of soldiers began to plunder the contents of the basement and the store shelves, the captain accused, "You said your family left. Who is upstairs?"

Before Joseph had time to reply, two armed soldiers ran up the flight of stairs where they discovered the elderly couple sipping tea.

"Young man, put down that gun!" Mrs. Peterson scolded. "My husband is not well."

"Sorry, mam. We thought you were Union soldiers."

"If I was forty years younger, I would be!" Mr. Peterson declared.

As the two Rebel soldiers laughed and returned downstairs, the two Union soldiers hiding in a closet gave a sigh of relief.

* * *

As lines of infantry passed by the Gunther's farm, Emma, her sister-in-law Elizabeth and niece Maggie were busy in the kitchen baking biscuits.

"Henry, grab some buckets and come with me to the well. These men need water!" Uncle John invited.

"Yes, sir!" the lad replied, relieved to be out of the kitchen with the ladies.

"Do be careful!" Emma fretted.

"Yes, mam." He was proud to do a man's job with his favorite uncle.

When Emma heard a nearby explosion, she looked out the window and saw a soldier flying in the air. Two other soldiers picked him up and headed toward the house.[3]

"Mercy! Elizabeth, we have company!" she informed her sister-in-law as she wiped the flour off her hands and ran out the back door. Elizabeth cleared off her dining room table and instructed Maggie to rip up some old sheets.

Emma gasped when she saw the badly wounded and burned soldier near the door. "Right through here," she directed the trio into the dining room. "Maggie, perhaps you should leave," she instructed her niece.

"No, Mam. This poor man is injured and needs our help. We need a basin of clean water and bandages," Maggie instructed.

This soldier was the first of scores to arrive that Wednesday. As the daylight decreased, the numbers of the wounded brought to the farm increased.

* * *

By now Isaac Miller was no stranger to death and war. But never had he witnessed such carnage! Sitting in the relative safety of the dark, he bit into his hard tack.

"Isaac Miller, is that you?"

"Monroe? You survived!"

"Yeah. Is David with you?" he asked anxiously.

"No. I thought he was with you."

"Do you think he is somewhere out there?" Monroe nodded to the darkened battlefield strewn with the dead and dying.

"I think he has been separated from the regiment in all of this chaos. We will find him tomorrow," Isaac attempted to sound confident.

"Do you really think so?"

"I really hope so, Monroe."

"Isaac, I have never seen anything like this," his voice trembled.

"Hopefully, we never will."

* * *

On Thursday, July 2 sharpshooter Darian Flynn shifted his weight on the tree limb where he was precariously balanced. By now most of his fellow sharpshooters traded their green uniforms for the anonymity of the Union blue. Many felt their green uniforms made them an easy target of the Confederates' wrath. Not Darian. He defiantly wore his green uniform, blending in with the leaves. Yesterday he had witnessed the slaughter of hundreds of men from his perch in the tree.

As he prayed the battle would mercifully end today, he glanced down and saw some familiar faces of the 17th Regiment of Maine below him. He forced himself to look away and stare through the sight of his rifle. After twenty minutes he looked down again and saw Isaac collapsed on the ground screaming as he held his left leg.

Darian had witnessed scenes like this countless of times. He had seen firsthand the damage a Minnie ball, a cone shaped bullet made from lead, could do when it flattened as it encountered human flesh. The deformed bullet would tear a terrible swath through bone and tissue. The bones would splinter into hundreds of sharp bony sticks that were driven by the force of the bullet.[4] He knew Isaac's only chance of survival was amputation.

Darian did the unthinkable – he flung his rifle over one shoulder, shimmied down the tree and left his post to rescue his friend. He knelt by Isaac, "It's me! It's Darian! You will be alright. Let me help you stand up." He lifted Isaac over his other shoulder and staggered to the long line of injured who were headed toward a large white farmhouse in the distance.

* * *

By Thursday morning, the soldiers were helping themselves to the Gunther's well. Henry was free to help Uncle John and some soldiers carry the dead bodies out of the house and carefully place them as far as safely possible from the house. When two soldiers were shot dead while standing in the back yard, Uncle John sent him to the house to help the ladies.

By the afternoon, every available space on the floor or on the furniture in the home was occupied by the wounded. Amputated limbs began to pile up outside of the house. Henry and the ladies had ripped every sheet, blanket, towel, curtains and even petticoats for bandages.

John Gunther directed the wounded to his now empty barn. Most of his livestock escaped the night before when the soldiers tore down his fences for campfires. Some were slaughtered and roasted to feed the famished troops. Marching infantry and cavalry had torn up all his fields. His crops were a total loss.

He summoned Henry to report to the barn to assist the surgeons. While crossing the yard, he spotted a green uniform carrying a wounded soldier. A sharpshooter! Henry had heard about them, but he had never seen one before.

"Over here! To the barn!" Henry called to Darian. "It is not safe in the yard! Rebels are firing at us from over there!"

For the first time Darian experienced the same dread he had caused countless of Rebels as he hurried into the barn. To his dismay the floor was littered with the dead and dying. An assortment of gruesome amputated limbs piled up in a corner. A surgeon splattered in blood held a knife between his teeth as he sutured a patient. Soldiers with shattered limbs lay on the floor waiting for their turn.[5]

Doctors set up all manners of tables to treat the wounded. Surgeons used benches, barrels covered with planks and doors taken off their hinges as tables for surgery.[6]

"No, Darian!" Isaac begged.

"Do you want to see Lydia and the girls again? This is the only way."

Isaac held on tighter. "Tell Lydia I am sorry. I should have been a better husband. Promise me when you get home, you will watch out for them. Don't let my little girls forget me."

"You can tell her yourself. You don't need two legs to care for your family."

The nurse came over with a dirty rag dipped in chloroform. "I must return to my post," Darian explained. "I will be back tomorrow. I promise."

As Isaac mercifully drifted into unconsciousness, Darian reluctantly left the barn.

Isaac was one of the lucky ones for he had a space in the barn. As the daylight decreased, the number of wounded soldiers increased. Since both buildings were already overcrowded the new arrivals were placed outside on the ground surrounding the farmhouse.[7]

That night Monroe Quint frantically searched for both David and Isaac. Discouraged, he sat down on the ground and took out his pocket New Testament. He read a few verses from the Gospel of John, before closing his eyes and falling asleep clutching the Book.

As the sun rose on Friday, July 3 neither the Union nor Confederate soldiers realized it would be the last day of battle at Gettysburg. For Monroe Quint it would be his final battle when he was killed in an artillery bombardment.[8]

* * *

Darian kept his promise and returned to the Gunther's barn that evening. He found Isaac laying listlessly on a dirty blanket with a bloody bandage on his stump. He slumped down by his friend. "We won."

Isaac grunted in acknowledgment. "Have you seen David and Monroe?"

Darian shook his head. "It is chaos out there," he pointed to the battlefield. "But I will search every nook and cranny here to see if they have been wounded." Isaac drifted off to sleep.

The next morning, Saturday July 4, Henry shyly approached the sharpshooter. "How is your friend?"

"I fear he is dying. Is there any way I could get a letter home to his family?"

"If you could visit Gunther's Mercantile on West Middle Street and tell my father that the family is well, I am sure he will supply you with pen and paper and mail your letter."

"Happy Fourth of July," Darian greeted, relieved to see that Isaac had lived through the night. "I am going into town to write and mail a letter home. Danny will come to take you home. You will be with Lydia and the girls before you know it." He hoped he sounded confident. Isaac merely grunted.

Darian wearily headed into town in the pouring rain. Most of the citizens of Gettysburg had slept through the Confederate's overnight retreat and were awakened by the arrival of Federal troops.[9] However, soldiers and civilians alike were still in danger of gunfire from Seminary Hill for General Robert E. Lee had not yet begun his retreat from the area.[10]

The Confederates had built a barricade across Baltimore Street from confiscated furniture in nearby homes.[11] He found Gunther's Mercantile and politely knocked on the front door which had been torn off its hinges. A middle-aged man quickly opened it.

"Mr. Gunther, I have a message from Henry."

"Is my family all right?" he asked anxiously.

"Your family is safe. The ladies worked tirelessly baking biscuits until they ran out of flour and fed the troops until they ran out of food. Henry spent days giving water to passing troops at great risk to himself. He has assisted doctors and nurses in the care of the wounded and dying and brought comfort and kindness to hundreds. It may be prudent to remain there until all hostilities have ceased. But he asked me to inform you that the entire family is well."

"Oh, thank God! Is there anything I may do to repay you for this kindness?"

"There is one, sir. May I have a pen and paper to write home? My best friend is dying, and I want to write to his family." He quickly scribbled a note and addressed the envelope.

"I will take it to the post office myself," Joseph promised.

"Thank you, sir." Darian left the store and headed back down Baltimore Street. He never returned to Gunther's Farm.

VIII

The Reporter

Gettysburg, Sunday, July 5, 1863

Thaddeus Pierce did not believe in heaven; he would soon believe in hell. He was traveling on a train to Gettysburg to report on the newly created, efficient army medical care. Dr. Jonathan Letterman, medical director of the Army of the Potomac, revolutionized battlefield treatment. Each division established a field hospital in the rear of the unit – far enough away to be out of danger, yet near enough so ambulances could deliver their wounded. Letterman's plan was so detailed it included setting up cook tents, organizing food, water and medical supplies to the hospitals.

His plan included field hospitals with a fully equipped ambulance corps to serve them. Each regiment had its own ambulance and every brigade, division and corps had officers responsible for the ambulance service. Each brigade had its own medicine and supply wagons. Six hundred and fifty Union doctors were ready to treat the wounded.[1] It was a genius plan and Pierce was here to document every detail.

The train came to an abrupt halt. "This is not Gettysburg," Thaddeus complained to the conductor.

"The Rebels took out the only train track to Gettysburg days ago This is the end of the line," he explained wearily.[2]

Cursing under his breath, he grabbed his leather valise, and stepped down into the depot. "Where am I?" he wondered out loud.

"This is York," a man sitting in a nearby wagon explained.

"How am I supposed to get to Gettysburg?"

"Why would anyone in their right mind want to go to Gettysburg?" he questioned suspiciously.

"I am a reporter for the New York Post on assignment. Could I pay you to give me a ride?" he asked hopefully.

"Suit yourself. Put your bag in back and hop in. As soon as I mail this letter, I am returning to Gettysburg anyway."

"You live in Gettysburg?"

"My whole life."

Thaddeus could not believe his good fortune. He could interview an eyewitness while traveling to his destination. "Why did you come all the way out here to mail a letter?"

"It's a matter of life and death for one poor soldier. There is no mail service. The Rebels destroyed the telegraph lines and all three of our newspapers are shut down. We are totally isolated from the rest of the world. No one knows what we have experienced."[3]

"Tell me and soon the whole world will know," he bragged. "My name is Thaddeus Pierce," he handed the driver a business card.

"Joseph Gunther."

"Did you witness any fighting? Did you see any medical staff caring for the wounded?"

"Those dirty Rebels stole everything from my shop. It is a good thing that I hid my horse in the woods. I could not believe it when he returned home last night in the rain. I sent my family to my brother's farm to be safe. I don't think anyone was safe for those three days. I took in some elderly neighbors and hid two Union soldiers. Once the Rebels cleared out, they left. But then I took in a seriously wounded soldier from Minnesota. I heard a local girl was killed by a Reb. Shot through the heart. This happened at her sister's house, not in our neighborhood," he clarified.

"What was this girl's name?" Now that's a story you do not hear every day. A Northern woman being killed by a Confederate soldier. Perhaps he should pursue this lead.

"Jenny Wade."[4]

"Why did you take in a wounded soldier? Would he not receive better care at the field hospital?" Thaddeus suspected that this man was exaggerating.

"What field hospitals?" he demanded. "Every church in town is a hospital. Our new courthouse is a hospital, our public school."

"Where is Dr. Letterman?"

"Who? Folks put up red flags on their doors to show wounded soldiers could come in for care.[5] So I took in a wounded soldier. No one has seen any sign of a doctor or a bandage for that matter."

The muddy, rutted roads made for slow travel. Finally, they arrived at the center of town, which Mr. Gunther called the Diamond, where all the roads converged. They were greeted by silence. Dazed town's people cautiously left their homes and aimlessly wandered their neighborhood. Neighbors quietly greeted one another comparing their experiences in hushed towns. Even the soldiers whispered to one another.[6]

Thaddeus gave his companion two silver dollars. "Thank you for the ride and the information, Mr. Gunther."

The reporter's first stop was at a warehouse at the corner of Baltimore and Middle Streets near the Diamond. The U.S. Sanitation Commission just arrived with five wagons of supplies.[7]

"What do you have here?" Thaddeus inquired.

"Medical supplies, blankets, food. We are expecting tents soon," the worker explained as he began unloading the first wagon.

"Why? The army will take care of that," Thaddeus argued.

"Do you mean the army that has six hundred and fifty doctors and taking five hundred and forty-four with them to the next battle?"

"But that only leaves one hundred and six doctors for… How many wounded?"

"No one knows. They are spread out all over town. Thousands. Maybe ten thousand. That is just Union soldiers. We have no idea how many wounded Confederate soldiers were left behind."

"How will Dr. Letterman manage?"

"He is leaving tomorrow morning with the army. I understand that Dr. Janes is in charge. I hope he gets those tents. There are hundreds of wounded laying on the ground out in the open in the hot sun and in the pouring rain. Men have been without food for days. The wagons with blankets, tents and basic hospital supplies are nowhere in sight."[8]

"I do not believe it."

"Do not take my word for it. See for yourself," he shrugged as he carried the first of many loads into the warehouse.

Down the street he met delegates from the U.S. Christian Commission moving supplies into their warehouse in Schick's store on the central square.[9] "Do you have any tents? I understand there are hundreds of wounded outside in the elements," Thaddeus informed.

"We are unloading food. With the Lord's help, tomorrow morning we will begin distributing food to our soldiers and any families who have taken in soldiers. We are expecting more delegates every day who will bring donated supplies. We are recruiting doctors to come to care for the wounded soldiers. All soldiers. It matters not to us the color of their uniforms."

"Do you mean civilian doctors? Will the army allow civilians to care for the soldiers?"

"Do they have a choice? I hear rumors that most of the doctors are leaving tomorrow leaving about a hundred to treat thousands. I heard there are 14,000 wounded. That is Union soldiers. Thousands of wounded confederates have been abandoned."[10]

Could you help us unload?"

Thaddeus shook his head. "I am a reporter to investigate battlefield medical care."

"Perhaps you may investigate the number of wounded and where they are located? That would help us with our distributions."

Thaddeus' first stop was the Adams County Court House which was crowded with wounded soldiers laying on the wooden floors. The court room now served as the operating room.[11] As he began silently counting, a harried doctor rushed in.

"Do you know how many patients are here?" Thaddeus thought that was a reasonable question. All he had to do was to visit the hospitals and add up the numbers.

"Have no idea. They are arriving almost as fast as they are dying," he rushed by.

His next stop was the two-story brick public school on East Street where he found similar crowded and filthy conditions. The first floor was reserved for Union soldiers while the second floor held Confederates.[12]

The scene was the same in every church in town with no food, beds, or clean bedding. The pastor of Christ Lutheran church told Thaddeus, "There are hundreds more at Pennsylvania College and our Seminary. These are the fortunate ones. No one knows how many are still left on the battlefields."

He slowly headed toward the Seminary. Suddenly overwhelmed by the stench of decaying flesh, flies, heat, thirst and hunger, he vomited by the side of the road. He sat down to rest against a bullet ridden tree. He slowly looked up to meet the vacant stare of a badly mangled body precariously dangling from an overhead branch.

He wearily grabbed his valise, got up and continued toward the Seminary. He looked neither to the left nor to the right even when he heard groans or screams. He stepped over the bodies lying across his path.

To distract himself from the horrors, he began writing his articles in his head. Without access to a telegraph, he would have to return to his Washington office first thing tomorrow morning.

He staggered into the Lutheran Theological Seminary where doctors heroically treated the hundreds of wounded. "Where are your medical supplies?" Thaddeus asked an exhausted doctor with dried blood on the front of his white shirt.

"The Confederates confiscated most of our surgical tools.[13] We have at least twenty more amputations. You will just have to do the best you can with the instruments you brought," he nodded to the valise.

"You do not expect me to operate!"

"Well, that is why you came here, is it not?"

"I am not a doctor. I am a reporter for the New York Post."

"Well, here is your story," he said angrily." Hundreds wounded, hundreds dying. No food, no water, no medical supplies and I just received orders I am shipping out tomorrow. Who will care for these poor souls? If you are not a doctor, you must leave."

"May I talk with some of the soldiers?"

"No! Leave my patients alone. Go out to the battlefield to interview those soldiers. Ask them how long they were lying there. Go interview General Meade and ask him where are our medical supplies? The last thing I need is some reporter gawking at my patients. Now leave!" he shouted.

A soldier appeared and escorted him out the back door. Thaddeus observed a blackened hand protruding from a shallow grave. "That is no way to bury a body!" he accused.

"How do you propose to dig thousands of graves without a shovel?" the soldier snapped.

"I am sorry. How many bodies have you buried?"

"Today?"

"No. I mean in total. I am trying to estimate the number of dead and wounded."

"I stopped counting," he shrugged.

Thaddeus sat on the grass and took out his notebook. He reviewed his notes and added more details. He had seen thousands of abandoned muskets, blankets and knapsacks littering the fields. He estimated the value of all this government property to be in the millions of dollars.[14] He wondered how many of those guns were still loaded. With the army leaving tomorrow, it would be easy for remaining Confederate soldiers to gather these weapons to bring back to the enemy or to kill wounded soldiers and civilians.

By now it was early evening and Thaddeus was determined to reach his next destination. He heard a horse and wagon slow down behind him. "Sir, I will pay $2.00 if you will take me to Pennsylvania College."

"Are you a doctor?" the elderly driver inquired.

"No. I am a reporter for the New York Post," he explained as he took two silver dollars and a business card from his pocket.

"I guess I can give you a ride," he took the coins. "If you were a doctor, I would have done it for free."

The wagon stopped in front of a four-story building. "Why do you want to visit the Confederate hospital?" A Federal soldier guarding the front door asked suspiciously.

"I was not aware this is a Confederate hospital" He took out his business card. "Thaddeus Pierce, reporter from the New York Post."

"These patients are prisoners of war. I will not let you pass."

"Fair enough. Perhaps you could answer a few questions for me and then I will be on my way." He was not going to pay $2.00 to get here and not learn any new information.

"How did this become a Confederate hospital? Did our army capture them and bring them here?"

"When the enemy drove us out of town, they began bringing their wounded here. They filled up every room and corridor. When the enemy retreated, they left the wounded behind with a few doctors to care for them."

"How many wounded?"

"Over seven hundred."[15]

"How many dead?"

"Not enough."

Night was rapidly falling as Thaddeus Pierce made his way back to the center of town. Every moan and shriek from the abandoned battle fields terrified him and he quickened his pace. As he approached the town, nothing looked familiar in the dark and he doubted he had arrived at the Diamond. Then he spotted lights in the windows of the Wagon Hotel.

He was ten paces from the front door when he heard a crack and his hat blew off. He heard another crack and a dead Confederate soldier fell off the roof.

"It is not safe to be out after dark," a voice warned as a young soldier appeared from the shadows.

Observing his uniform Thaddeus commented, "Private, I see you are from Maine."

"Yup."

He suddenly felt homesick. "I grew up in Maine. Where are you from?"

The soldier disappeared into the night without reply.

Trembling, he entered the hotel, rented a space on the floor and collapsed in exhaustion.

* * *

He returned to the U.S. Christian Commission office the next morning. "How may we help you?" The delegate did not recognize this disheveled man in a dusty and stained suit to be the same self-important reporter from yesterday.

"I promised that I would return today and report my findings."

"Yes, I remember. Mr. Pierce."

"I would estimate that each church in town is holding two hundred wounded soldiers. No one has beds, blankets, enough food or adequate medical supplies. It appears that the Seminary is in the greatest need of all. The Confederates took their medical supplies before their retreat.

The most pressing need is shovels. They need hundreds of shovels."

"Shovels? Why would doctors need shovels?"

"To properly bury the dead. There are bodies everywhere rotting in the sun, and those that have been buried are in shallow graves where animals can dig them up. There are hundreds of dead horses and mules attracting swarms of flies. Something must be done before an outbreak of pestilence."

"The magnitude of destruction has surpassed our expectations. The telegraphs are down. I must return to Baltimore immediately to report your findings. Shovels. Yes shovels. How can I thank you for your report?"

"Take me to Baltimore and we will call it even."

IX

The Arrival

Fryeburg, July 11, 1863

As Rachel was sorting the U.S. mail, she spied the letter from Darian addressed to Daniel. "Peter, Darian was in Gettysburg. You know the town in Pennsylvania that had the bloody battle last week."

"According to the newspaper it sounds like everyone was fighting in Gettysburg and the town is in dire need of basic supplies. The store will not open for another hour, perhaps you should deliver it to Danny now," he suggested.

With the letter in one hand and her bonnet in the other she dashed out the door to Isaac's house. She was relieved to see Daniel's horse in the stable. She knocked on the back door and entered to find the family dressed and eating breakfast.

"Darian wrote you a letter from Gettysburg," she handed the correspondence to her brother and waited patiently for him to read it.

Dear Danny,

Isaac was shot in the leg on Thursday and the surgeon had to amputate it. He is in the barn at John Gunther's farm on Taneytown Road. There are thousands dead and even more wounded. He will surely die if you do not come with clean bedding, clothes, bandages, food and medicine. His brother, Joseph Gunther on West Middle Street will take you there.

Darian

"Girls, please go upstairs to play with your dolls." No one had to ask Mahayla twice to go play.

"Is he dead?" Lydia asked fearfully. "Will I have to raise my children without a father?"

"He has been seriously wounded and in need of our family's help. My mother will know what to pack and I will leave this afternoon."

Lydia sobbed, "I told him that I did not want him to go. I begged him, but he would not listen."

"Danny, I will accompany you to Gettysburg," Emily offered.

"Please don't leave me too. I need you here!" Lydia begged.

Daniel agreed, "You need to remain with Lydia and the girls. That is what Isaac would want. I could be away for days or weeks. Stay here while Rachel and I go tell my parents."

Daniel and Rachel found their parents with Eli in the barn. "What is wrong?" Kate asked. "The two of you would not be here unless…" she could not finish the sentence.

"Ma, Isaac was shot in the leg last week and the doctor had to amputate."

Kate covered her mouth with both hands and stifled a sob as Jacob protectively put his arm around her shoulder.

"Was he shot in that town in Pennsylvania that had the big battle? What hospital is he in? We should go visit him at once." Jacob declared.

"Pa, I think it will be best for you to stay home. Danny will go," Eli stated firmly.

"I agree, Pa. Although I would appreciate the company, I fear the journey would be too taxing. According to Darian's letter, the surgery took place in a barn. I do not know what hospital he is in or even if he is in a hospital."

"A barn? Gracious! I have never heard of such a thing!" Kate exclaimed.

"Mama, all I know is what I read in the newspapers," Rachel began. "The Rebels stole all the food. Churches, schools, private homes are serving as hospitals. According to the article, they lack the most basic supplies."

Kate abruptly headed to the house and entered the kitchen with the others quickly following. She grabbed a large canvas bag from the pantry and began filling it with cloth bandages, teas, soap and salves. She went to the linen cupboard and took two pairs of sheets. "Have Lydia pack some of his clothes."

"You can catch the stagecoach at the Oxford Hotel to Portland. There is one leaving in two hours. From there you can take a train to Boston and then to New York. From New York go to Philadelphia. If you cannot get to Gettysburg from there, try traveling further south to Baltimore," Rachel instructed.

Daniel looked at his sister in amazement. "How do you know this?"

"The store receives shipments by rail all the time. I could come with you," she offered for everyone knew Daniel's discomfort in traveling.

"Thank you. I would appreciate your company. However, your family needs you and I do not know how long I will be away.

Eli took his brother aside. "Isaac could already be dead, you know."

Daniel had not thought of that. "Then I shall take care of someone else's brother."

* * *

Daniel was hot, hungry, thirsty and thoroughly agitated. The cities and trains were noisy, crowded and dirty. Eli would have known how to deal with the crowds and talk to strangers. Eli was able to meet any challenge and take control of any situation. Why did he not volunteer instead?

The constant racket of the locomotives made his head throb. The conductor assured him it was just one more hour.

Panic began to set in. Would he be able to find the Gunther residence? Would he be able to find Isaac? What if he is already dead? How would he find his brother's grave? The newspaper articles said the dead were buried everywhere. How would he bring his brother's body home?

He silently prayed, "Dear Lord, you led the Israelites out of Egypt and parted the Red Sea. You led them by a cloud by day and by fire by night. Please guide me for I know not where to go or what to do. Please help me to stop thinking about my situation and to serve others." He looked at his fellow passengers and wondered how many of them were also seeking a loved one.

His peace of mind was short lived when the train pulled into the station. There were groups of wounded soldiers – many with crutches, some with bandages, a few with slings; all looked dirty and defeated. They had been waiting for hours in the sun to take the train out of Gettysburg to a hospital. Piles of caskets were lined up by the tracks.[1] Daniel did not know if they were filled with bodies to be returned home or empty waiting to be filled.

He remained in his seat as the other passengers exited. Grabbing his canvas bag, he stepped off the train, took a deep breath and gagged.

"You never grow accustomed to it," an elderly bystander commented.

"What is that stench?" he asked as he swatted flies away from his face.

"Death," he replied grimly.

"Are you searching for a loved one as well?"

"No. I have lived here all my life. There are folks from all over, looking for family – just like you. Who are you looking for?"

"My brother. The last I heard he was at the Gunther's farm. I have instructions to find Mr. Gunther's Mercantile on West Middle Street. Do you know where he lives?" he asked hopefully.

"Everyone knows Gunther's Mercantile."

"Excuse me, sir. Please forgive me for being forward," a middle-aged woman holding a parasol in one hand and a handkerchief to cover her nose with the other interrupted. I grew up in Gettysburg and I am here to take my parents home with me. I will show you the way and will be grateful for an escort."

"Thank you," Daniel let out an audible sigh of relief. Gettysburg appeared to be much larger than Fryeburg with a new courthouse, several churches of different denominations and a two-story school.

"All these buildings are temporary hospitals. As soon as a patient is well enough to move, they are shipped off to Washington or Baltimore. Of course, many of them have already died. I heard there are 14,000 wounded. Union soldiers, that is. Not rightly sure how many Confederates were left behind," the elderly bystander explained as he accompanied them.

Daniel's heart sank. How would he find Isaac? They walked through a crowded and chaotic center of town. "This is the Diamond. Before the battle we were a peaceful, prosperous town of 2,400. First, we were overrun with soldiers now we are overwhelmed by visitors. There are volunteers from all over to help and many people like you looking for relatives. Of course, some are here to gawk or to steal souvenirs from the battlefields. Here is West Middle Street. Hope you find your brother." The man turned around and disappeared into the crowd.

Daniel and the woman entered Gunther's Mercantile where they found the family and the Petersons rebuilding shelves.

"Nancy!" Mrs. Peterson cried and opened her arms.

"Mother, I am here to take the two of you home with me. Just until the war is over."

"I think that is a wise plan," Joseph agreed. "What would happen if you should fall ill? The few doctors here are caring for wounded and they do not have enough medicine for them. After we repair the store and reopen, we will begin to repair your house."

"Repair?" Nancy asked.

"They stole everything that was not nailed down," Mr. Peterson complained. Our windows are shattered."

"That settles it. We will pack your clothes, head back to the train station and take the first train back to Philadelphia," Nancy firmly stated.

"I will take the four of you in the wagon," Emma offered.

Daniel blushed. "Oh no, I am not her husband. I received a letter from Darian Flynn stating my brother has been shot and is staying at the Gunther Farm."

"The sharpshooter. That is his name, Darian?" Henry asked.

"You must be the brother from Maine. I was uncertain if you received the letter. The post office was closed for days. I had to go to York to mail it."

"First, let me thank you for doing so. I am sure it was under the most trying of circumstances. Could you kindly direct me to Mr. Gunther's farm?"

"Papa, I can take him to Uncle John's farm," Henry volunteered.

"First our guests will have some refreshments. I fear all I have to offer is tea and crackers," Emma apologized.

Daniel was humbled when he realized this generous family was offering a stranger everything they had. He opened his bag. "I have mint tea and chamomile," he handed her two cotton bags. I have half a loaf of bread and some blueberry preserves."

Henry's eyes widened. "This is most generous, Mr. ..." Emma began.

"Miller, Daniel Miller. I own a sawmill in Fryeburg, Maine. I am here searching for my brother, Private Isaac Miller, 17th Regiment of Maine. There is nothing I would rather do at this moment than share some of my food from home with all of you."

"Shall we go upstairs? Thank the good Lord, our home is still intact."

Daniel saw a soldier sitting in a parlor chair with a bandaged leg resting on a foot stool and a bandaged right shoulder.[2]

"Please forgive me for not standing."

"It is an honor to make your acquaintance, sir," Daniel walked over to the officer and shook his left hand. "Should you not be in a hospital?"

"Nonsense, we are giving him much better care here than one of those overcrowded, filthy, makeshift hospitals," Emma began before realizing the impact of those words on her guest. Flustered, she invited, "Please, Mr. Miller, take a seat. It will just be a moment."

"All the food is gone; the grocery stores were looted by the Rebels," Joseph explained. "If it was not for the arrival of the U.S. Christian Commission, there would be no food to be had. We are thankful. Our family is alive and uninjured, and our home is undamaged."

"This will be a feast," Mrs. Gunther smiled brightly as she brought out a platter of sliced bread and the teapot. "When we are finished, Henry will bring your bag to the spare bedroom," she invited.

"You are too kind. I do not wish to impose. Perhaps you could direct me to a hotel?"

"There are no vacancies anywhere. You are no imposition," Emma assured. Since Mr. and Mrs. Peterson are leaving, the room is free."

"You are too kind," Daniel repeated. "My family and I are most grateful. I read in the newspaper that most of the doctors left when the army pulled out. Who are caring for the thousands of wounded?"

"Every day more civilian doctors arrive by train. The nuns from the Order of Sisters of Charity from Emmitsburg, Maryland are caring for the wounded at the Seminary. The Patriot Daughters of Lancaster are caring for the wounded at the Lutheran Church on Chambersburg Street," Joseph explained.

Daniel put down his teacup. "I need to find for my brother."

"I fear you may not find him there," Joseph warned. "Most of them died or moved."

Daniel's heart sank. How would he ever find Isaac? Was he one of the soldiers with crutches waiting at the train station? Was his body in one of the coffins?

"Perhaps John and Elizabeth will know where the wounded were taken," Emma suggested.

"I will take you," Henry offered. "Don't worry, we will find him."

"I hope so."

X

The Search

As Henry escorted Daniel down Baltimore street he explained, "I talked with your brother twice before we returned home on Tuesday, the 7th. I knew the sharpshooter was worried about him, so I went to check in on him."

Daniel was relieved to hear that. "That was very kind of you."

"We all have to do our part."

"What are all those fires?" he pointed in the distance.

"They might still be burning the dead animals. There were thousands of dead horses and mules. Also, it is easier to burn all the amputated arms and legs than to bury them. There was a pile of limbs stacked in my uncle's side yard. The pigs got loose and started eating them. I guess you cannot blame them. Their barns and feed were destroyed, and they were starving."

Daniel felt queasy. Did a ravenous hog devour his brother's leg?

"But even so Aunt Elizabeth declared that such things are uncivilized. She was quite distraught that my cousin witnessed the amputations in the house and dead bodies in the yard."

Daniel always avoided the farm on butchering days. How could women and children see such brutality? How could the soldiers endure it? How could Isaac?

"This is Taneytown Road. It is not much further. I wonder if the farm has any water left. His well was awfully low. Soldiers need water to drink if they are going to fight."

"My father and brother are farmers. I know a farm needs plenty of water for crops and livestock," he sympathized.

"His wheat field and crops were all destroyed. His livestock were either killed or escaped when the soldiers tore down his fences."

Daniel did not know how to respond so he said nothing. The two of them walked silently until Henry announced, "See that white farmhouse? There's the barn."

A farmer who looked to be Daniel's age met them as they reached the barn.

"Henry, there is no one left in there," John Gunther explained.

"Were did they all go? The barn was crowded with soldiers last week," he questioned.

"Most of them died. A few were brought to make-shift hospitals," he explained.

"I am looking for my brother, Private Isaac Miller. He had his leg amputated in here. Do you know where…" he did not know how to complete the sentence. Where he was buried? Where he was relocated?

"Uncle John, this is the father of our sharpshooter. He came all the way from Maine, looking for his brother."

"I am sorry to meet you under these trying circumstances," the farmer wiped the sweat off his forehead with a dirty handkerchief. "Please forgive me for not inviting you in, but the missus would be mortified if anyone saw the present state of our house."

"Do you have water?" Henry asked.

"Barely a trickle. Not that I have any crops or livestock left to water. But it takes buckets of water and soap to wash the blood off the floors. I have not had the time to clean out the barn. I just locked the doors."

Daniel spied a woman peering through the window. "Aunt Elizabeth gave all her curtains, sheets and pillowcases to be cut into bandages. Even some of her aprons and petticoats," Henry explained.

"Do you have time to replant?" Daniel knew the growing season in Pennsylvania was longer than in Maine.

"It will be a long time before I step foot in there," he nodded in the direction of his battered wheat field. "Who knows what else I could find?"

"Sir, I am so sorry for your losses. Thank you for your sacrifices in helping our troops, for helping my brother."

The farmer nodded. "I am sorry that I could not be more help."

Daniel swallowed his disappointment. He had hoped to find Isaac today. Now he realized it could take days or weeks to learn of his whereabouts.

The men shook hands and Daniel and Henry headed back to town. "Tomorrow we will go to the Christian Commission. They may be able to help us. Or we can begin going from church to church until we find him. There are hundreds of people here looking for family members. It just takes time, that's all," he reassured.

"You and your family have been most kind."

"We all have to do our part," Henry reiterated as they headed back.

Daniel found Mrs. Gunther had the spare bedroom ready for him. He placed the large canvas bag on the floor, found a sheet of paper, ink and two metal pens and wearily wrote,

> *"Dear Family,*
>
> *Just a short note to inform you that I have safely arrived in Gettysburg. The Joseph Gunther family has graciously offered a room in their home while I search for Isaac. And you may write me at this address. There are no soldiers in the Gunther's barn and tomorrow I will begin my search in earnest.*
>
> *Rachel, please put on my account enough fabric to make sheets, pillowcases, tablecloths, petticoats and curtains for several rooms and mail them to Mrs. John Gunther on Taneytown Road.*
>
> *I covet your prayers for the thousands of wounded soldiers left here and for all the families struggling to*

survive after the battle. I will write you every night until I am home again.

Danny.

He fell fast asleep as soon as his head hit the pillow.

When Daniel came downstairs the next morning, he found Henry dressed and ready to leave the house. "Mother said I may escort you to the Christian Commission building."

"Mr. and Mrs. Gunther, I am overwhelmed by your hospitality. I fear my search may take much longer than I originally planned. Could you direct me to a hotel, for I do not wish to take advantage.

"We will not hear of it. You are welcome to stay here for as long as needed. We all need to do our part, Mr. Miller. The Christian Commission is in the large storehouse at Schick's store.[2] Henry will show you."

"What do they do?"

"Everything."

Henry led Daniel to the front entrance of the warehouse. "They will help you find your brother, Mr. Miller."

Daniel entered and looked at the long lines of people. "Are you a delegate from your hospital with your list of needed supplies?"[3] a kind, well dressed woman asked.

"No, mam. My name is Daniel Miller, from Fryeburg, Maine…"

"Welcome. We are so blessed to have you join us. Are you a doctor or a minister?"

"Neither. I own a sawmill and I am a church elder."

"That is close enough. Come with me and I will give you some New Testaments to distribute. We have hundreds of doctors arriving from all over the North to care for the wounded. But we do more than care for broken bodies, we care for the souls. We pray, read scripture, write letters to homes, hold their hands while they lay dying."

"I am searching for my brother, Private Isaac Miller. I was hoping you could help me find him."

"Mr. Miller, there are 14,000 wounded Union soldiers and 6,800 abandoned, wounded Confederate soldiers.[4] I am sorry we do not have a list of all the patients. Many die every day, some transfer to hospitals in Baltimore and Washington, some return to duty and the lucky ones go home.

"Yes mam. You have been most helpful. Are you a volunteer here?"

"I am a mother who came to bring home her son. Instead the Lord gave me the privilege of holding his hand while he entered his eternal home. There is no reason for me to return home now. Why should I not stay and help someone else's son?

May I suggest that you begin your search at St. Francis Xavier Catholic Church. You will find Father McGinnis to be most helpful."[4]

"I am so sorry for your loss."

"May the Lord be with you. I pray you may find your brother."

With renewed hope and a clean handkerchief dabbed with peppermint oil held to his nose, he walked up the street and stopped in front of a brick building with white double wooden doors. The church had three arched, clear glass windows on each side of the building and capped by a distinctive cupola housing a four-hundred-pound bell. It was outlined by a white picket fence.[5]

As he entered the church he was greeted with the now familiar stench of blood, sweat and rotting flesh.

"Praise be to God! You must be another delegate from the U.S. Christian Commission," a young priest pointed to the New Testaments Daniel held in his hand.

The priest's Irish brogue brought a smile to Daniel's face. "You must be Father McGinnis. I must confess that I was expecting someone much older. When did you arrive from Ireland?"

"Seven years ago, at the age of twenty-one. Became a priest three years ago and arrived in Gettysburg two years ago."[6]

"I am searching for my brother, Private Isaac Miller 17th Regiment of Maine. He was wounded and had his leg amputated in John Gunther's barn. But there are no more soldiers left there. I am going from hospital to hospital to find him. Can you help me?"

"Dr. William Norris just arrived from Lincoln General Hospital in Washington yesterday. We have two hundred patients here and he is compiling a list. He might be able to tell you if your brother is here," he pointed to the harried doctor across the room.

The wounded were crowded in the sanctuary and the gallery. Some were lying in the pews, others under the pews and many in the aisles. He carefully made his away across the church avoiding stepping on an injured soldier.

"Dr. Norris?"

"Did you get the supplies I asked for from the Christian Commission?" he asked gruffly without looking up.

"No sir. I am looking for my brother Isaac ..."

"Look at this chaos! No beds, no blankets, no medicines, not enough food. And you want to know if I have seen your brother!"

"May I be of assistance?" offered a stranger. "I am Reverend McCullough, a delegate from the Christian Commission. One of the nuns could help you. The Sisters of Charity are here from Emmitsburg, Maryland.[7] They know every patient they are nursing. Come with me," he instructed. "Please excuse Dr. Norris," the pastor whispered, "he just arrived, and he is trying his best to care for his patients under these most distressing circumstances."

"I see you have stopped at the US Christian Commission warehouse," he pointed to the New Testaments.

"Yes, sir. May I be of service while I am waiting?"

"We would be most grateful. Two other delegates and I are building bunks to get the patients off the floors. We are sweeping the wet, musty straw out of the building and bringing in fresh bedding.[8] Oh, Sister!" he motioned to a woman dressed in a long black habit and veil. "Do we have a patient here by the name of..."

"Private Isaac Miller from the 17th Regiment of Maine. He is my brother. And yes, I would be honored to help you." Daniel was grateful to be helping these unselfish men and women. They willingly left the comforts of their homes to help strangers; he selfishly left home to find his brother. He took a broom and began to sweep.

"Pa! Pa! is that you?" cried a delirious young soldier who looked to be David's age. Daniel looked at his emaciated, ashen face, put down his broom and sat on the filthy floor beside him. "Pa, I don't want to die alone."

"You are not alone, son," he replied gently. "We are in the Lord's house." He picked up a New Testament and turned to the Gospel of John, Chapter 14 "Let not your heart be troubled: ye believe in God, believe also in me. In my Father's house are many mansions: if it were not so, I would have told you. I go to prepare a place for you. You are not alone. I am here. But more importantly our Savior is here, and He is waiting for you in Heaven."

"I'm afraid I ain't goin to heaven, Pa. I've done things since I left home that I'm ashamed of."

"He knows all that. Remember the thief on the cross. He confessed his sins and confessed that Jesus is Lord. And Jesus said, 'On this day you will be with me in Paradise.' You just confess your sins and He will accept you just as you are."

"Just like the hymn we sang in church. Can you sing it to me?"

Daniel blushed. It is one thing to sing with an entire congregation, but it is another to sing in front of two hundred strangers. "We all do what we can," he thought and began to sing.

"Just as I am, without one plea,
But that thy blood was shed for me,
And that thou bidst me to come to thee,
O Lamb of God, I come, I come."
A few quiet voices throughout the sanctuary joined in.
"Just as I am, and waiting not
To rid my soul of one dark blot,
To thee whose blood can cleanse each spot,
O Lamb of God, I come, I come."

Father McGinnis, Reverend McCullough, the two USCC delegates and a young woman came over and joined in.

"Just as I am, though tossed about
With many a conflict, many a doubt,
Fighting and fears within, without,
O Lamb of God, I come, I come."

Several of the soldiers, including the young man whose hand Daniel was holding, joined in.

"Just as I am, poor wretched, blind;
Sight, riches, healing of the mind,
Yea, all I need in thee to find, O Lamb of God, I come, I come."[9]

A young woman introduced herself to Daniel, "I am Sallie Myers. I teach school and I am spending the summer in Gettysburg with my parents."[10]

"Sally! Sally, is that you?"

"Of course, it is. I told you I would be back today to write a letter to your family. You did not tell me you could sing," she sat on the floor beside him, straightened out her skirt and took out her paper and pen.

Daniel said nothing as he continued sweeping.

"Are you handy with a hammer?" Reverend McCollough asked.

"I know more about sawing wood, than nailing it but I think I could build a bunk or two," Daniel offered.

A nun approached him. "Mr. Miller, there are no Isaac Millers listed here. You know this is not a long-term hospital. Our goal is to care for our patients until they are well enough to be shipped to Baltimore or Washington. If you cannot find him in Gettysburg, you might try visiting those hospitals."

"Thank you. I would like to stay for the afternoon and build bunks. Where should I go tomorrow to search?"

"I would start at Christ Lutheran Church."

It was twilight when an exhausted Daniel returned to the Gunther's home.

"Did you find him?" Henry asked excitedly.

"No. I spent the day helping at the Catholic Church. Tomorrow I will visit the Lutheran Church."

"Mother saved you some bread. You must eat."

It was only then Daniel realized that he had not eaten all day. Did Isaac have enough to eat he wondered as he began a letter to Emily.

Dearest Emily,

How I long to be home with you, with plenty to eat and smelling the clean mountain air outdoors and the scent of fresh sawdust at the mill. I am truly ashamed of my selfishness and I wonder how I would respond if there had been a battle in Fryeburg.

I met my first Catholic priest. He is from Ireland and just a few years older than Darian. It makes me realize how much I miss him. I also met my first group of nuns who are very efficient nurses. I met a pastor who willingly left his home and church to tend to the physical and spiritual needs of the soldiers. I met a young schoolteacher not much older than Lydia who is spending her summer vacation tending to the wounded.

Isaac was not there, yet I felt compelled to sweep floors and build beds. Tomorrow I will go to the Lutheran church and then the Court House, and the School House and the College and the Seminary. Please tell Lydia and my parents that I will not stop looking.

Until tomorrow,

Yours,
Danny

* * *

Daniel's first stop was to the Catholic Church to check on the young soldier. He was willing to sing again, if the need arose. As he opened the front door, Miss Myers came out with tears streaming down her cheeks.

"He is dead. But thanks to you, he died in peace. I am going home to write his family a letter. Excuse me," she brushed by him and headed down the street.

Downcast, Daniel turned around and slowly headed to the U.S. Christian Commission warehouse.

"Did you find your brother?" The kind woman from yesterday greeted.

"No, mam. I am going to look in the Lutheran Church. I thought I would first pick up more New Testaments to distribute. If he is not there, I will stay if they need any help."

"I am sure they will be grateful for any assistance."

He easily found the brick church, with three columns surrounded by a white picket fence on Chambersburg Street just west of the Diamond. [11]

"Are you a delegate from the Christian Commission?" asked a woman leaving her home across the street.

"No, mam. I am searching for my brother. But I stop by the Christian Commission in the mornings to pick up these," he held up several New Testaments.

"My name is Mary McCallister."

"Daniel Miller. Mrs. McCallister, I noticed that there are two Lutheran churches in town."

"This one speaks English. The other Lutheran church still speaks German. This church is affiliated with the Seminary and Pennsylvania College."

"Are they hospitals too?"

"Yes. But this church was the first public building in town to be commandeered as a hospital. It was a Union hospital behind enemy lines."[12]

"How did that happen?"

"On the first day of battle, the street was filled with retreating wounded Union soldiers with no place to go. I secured the keys from the sexton, opened the doors and the wounded flooded in. My friends tore up sheets for bandages. Every pew was filled with soldiers, sitting, lying or leaning on others. The dead were laid on a platform covered with sheets. Then the Rebels came." they retreated on July 3.[13] Otherwise all these men would now be prisoners of war."

"Who is in charge in here?"

"The doctors would like to think that they are. It is the Patriot Daughters of Lancaster who are providing meals and comfort.[14] They would know if your brother is in there."

"Thank you." He could feel his heart racing as he opened the front door. The nave held about one hundred soldiers. Boards were placed on top of pews for beds. The lecture hall on the ground floor held another forty patients. Next to this room was a makeshift operating room which smelled of blood and ether.

"Sir, may I help you?" a woman with an air of authority asked.

"Yes. Is there a patient named Isaac Miller, 17th regiment of Maine here? He had a leg amputated at someone's barn and he has been moved."

She checked a list. "You say he was transferred here?"

"No, mam. I do not know where he is. I am searching every hospital."

"He could be in someone's home or has been shipped by train to a hospital or…We have patients leaving soon for the train depot. Some will need assistance. If you care to help us, you will see patients from all the other hospitals waiting to depart as well."

"Mam, I would be honored to help."

"Follow me. Stephan, this is Mr.…"

"Miller. Daniel Miller. I am going to walk with you to the train station," he explained to the man who had bandages covering both eyes.

"I should have died," he said bitterly. "I am glad that I will not see the disappointment in my father's eyes when he learns of my injuries. I am the only son and my father expects me to take over his print shop. What purpose do I have in life now?"

"Where are you from?"

"Massachusetts."

"There is a school in Boston called the Perkins Institute for the Blind. They teach students how to read and write in Braille. I have read about Braille in a newspaper. It sounds like it is an alphabet made of raised dots that you can feel with your fingertips."

"You mean like Morse code?"

"I fear you are not the only soldier who has lost his sight in this terrible war. Plus, there are children and elderly people who are blind. You could become a teacher or write and print books in Braille."

"My grandmother is blind."

"Perhaps once you learn to read and write, you could teach her."

"My family does not know."

"You could dictate a letter to me, and I will write them."

"I have nothing to say."

"I have plenty to say. I have pen, ink and some paper." He pulled out his supplies and began.

> *I am writing on behalf of your son, Stephan. He fought very gallantly in the Battle of Gettysburg in Pennsylvania and was seriously wounded. The Patriot Daughters of Lancaster took very good care of him at Christ Lutheran Church which is serving as a military hospital.*

"That line is good, so my mother will not worry."

"Stephan, your mother has worried about you every day since you left home."

> *The good news is your son is well enough to leave this temporary hospital and will be taking the afternoon train out of Gettysburg. Thousands of soldiers have suffered serious injuries. My own brother had his*

leg amputated. Stephan has lost his sight, but not his spirit. I believe that good food and rest will strengthen his body.

He will have someone write you when he arrives at his next destination.

Sincerely yours,
Daniel Miller
Fryeburg, Maine

"I will address this letter and mail it at the post office on the way to the train station."

"May I use your pen and paper to write my wife? She has not heard from me in a while and I am sure she and the children will be getting worried," another soldier asked.

"Could you write a letter for me to my family?" a soldier with an empty right sleeve asked.

The next hour was devoted to letter writing followed by a lunch prepared and served by the Patriot Daughters. Daniel was grateful when they offered him a bowl of soup and a slice of bread.

A group of patients, two nurses, three volunteers from the Christian Commission and Daniel made a slow procession to the train station. They made three stops – two to rest and one at the post office where Daniel deposited five letters.

"Stephan, sit here," Daniel helped him to a bench. I need to search the crowd for my brother. He returned to the bench when he heard a train whistle in the distance.

"Did you find him?"

"No. But it is only my third day here."

"Mr. Miller -"

"Danny," he interrupted. "My friends and family call me Danny."

"Danny, I do not know how to thank you."

"You can thank me by finding the purpose in your life and have your parents write me. I put my address as the return address."

Two exhausted nurses walked by carrying a patient with no legs.

"Excuse me, could the two of us carry him onto the train? Daniel volunteered.

"But I can't see," Stephan protested.

"But I can. And you can walk," the double amputee observed wryly.

With a concerted effort, the three managed to enter the train. The nurses helped the two soldiers get comfortable in their seats.

Stephan did not see Daniel waving goodbye as the train headed to Washington.

That evening Daniel wrote

Dear Family,

No sign of Isaac. This scrap of paper is the last piece I have. Please mail me paper, bottles of ink, pens and stamps. Mahayla, thank you for your drawing of the flowers in Nana's garden. I will not leave until I find Isaac. I miss you all.

Danny.

XI

Camp Letterman

Daniel entered the Christian Commission warehouse to pick up his New Testaments. After spending a week and half visiting churches, the courthouse, the school and the seminary, he was uncertain of his next move. There was no word from the hospitals in Baltimore and Washington, nor official notification of his death. He could not give up and go home. He was now determined that he would canvas every home and barn in Gettysburg.

"Mr. Miller, I have been waiting for you! Have you heard the news? The Medical Director of the Union Army of the Potomac, Dr. Jonathan Letterman, is establishing one large military hospital for all the wounded. Every wounded soldier in churches, schools, homes and barns will be transported to one hospital. If your brother is alive, you will find him there. In fact, we are moving our headquarters there," the volunteer excitedly explained.

"Where is this hospital?" Daniel asked eagerly as he silently thanked the Lord for this good news.

"They have eighty acres at George Wolf's farm along the York Pike. I heard they are setting up four hundred hospital tents. There will be a cook house, dining tent, a surgical tent, living quarters for the medical staff. The U.S. Sanitation Commission and we will have our own tents. The camp is by the railroad. Supplies can be easily delivered, and patients can be easily transported.[1]"

"May I help the Commission pack and move?"

"I was counting on it," she laughed.

Daniel drove the wagon filled with crates down York Road and turned onto the entrance lane to the camp. To his right he passed the springs. There would be plenty of clean water to drink and to wash.

"Those are the dining tents and way over there is the cook house."

"There sure are a lot of tents," Daniel observed.

"They have to feed over four thousand patients, plus all the medical staff and volunteers. Those tents to our left are the sleeping quarters for the camp support staff and surgeons."

He returned his gaze to the right as he passed a sea of tents lined in rows in military precision. "Are these the hospital ward tents?"

"Yes. There are four hundred tents with ten patients in a tent. Here is our tent waiting to be filled," she pointed excitedly.

Daniel helped her down and looked around. "What are those tents way over there by themselves?"

"That one is the dead house and the other is the embalming tent. The field behind it will be the hospital cemetery."

"Why have an embalming tent when the cemetery is only a few yards away?"

"It is for the families who want to take their loved ones' remains home. For many it will be a long wagon or train ride."[2]

Daniel stood in the lane with his hands on his hips and declared, "I have never seen anything like this!"

"That is because nothing like this has ever existed before," a familiar voice behind him answered.

"Reverend McCoulough! You are still here?"

"Indeed, I am and so are you I see," he observed. "Have you led any more hymn sings?"

Daniel shook his head, "Letter writing, Bible reading, praying, listening, scrubbing floors, burying the dead but no singing."

"Well, once the patients arrive, we will hold services and you can lead the singing. After we have supplied the Christian Commission's tent, perhaps the two of us can help set up the cots. I understand the army is expecting the shipment to arrive by rail this afternoon. Over the next week there will be shipments of bedding, sheets, blankets."

"Gladly! The sooner the hospital is ready, the sooner the patients can arrive and the sooner I will find my brother."

"They even built a new train depot to unload supplies and to transfer patients"

That evening back in his room he excitedly wrote his family.

July 17th, 1863
My Dearest Family,

How I miss each one of you every day. Thank you for the pens and paper. Rachel, please send me every sheet of paper, every pen, ink, ink well and sealing wax you have in stock! Mama, please send as much tea and soap you can spare. Pa, please ask Reverend Sewall if the church can take up a collection of men's clothing and mail it to the U.S. Christian Commission. Size and style do not matter.

The army is constructing a massive military hospital consisting of tents. It is the most incredible sight and when I return home, I will describe it in detail. Within the week doctors, nurses and volunteers will transfer patients from every building, home and barn to this one centralized hospital. This is the answer to my prayers. I feared I would spend several more weeks visiting every house in town in my search. Now Isaac will be brought here.

Mama, I do apologize for writing such short letters. I fear the heat and exhaustion gets the better of me by the end of the day and I write few words. I promise I will be filled with stories about all the extraordinary people I have met who have faced such adversity with strength and courage. There are other stories which shall never be told, and I pray that someday I shall be able to forget. But tonight, I am encouraged.

*Always,
Danny*

Daniel spent the next week unloading crates from trains, making beds, stocking shelves in the Christian Commission's supply tent. Patients began to arrive by stretcher, wagon and carriage in a haphazardly fashion. Four double amputees arrived by hearse, causing great excitement when the nurse opened the door. However, patients at the public school and the Seminary remained in those hospitals for several weeks longer.

While Daniel was stocking items with his coworkers, Reverend McCoulough burst into the Christian Commission's tent. "Come with me. I found your brother!"

Daniel dropped his supplies and ran out of the tent followed by three rejoicing women. "It is truly a miracle. An answer to our prayers!"

Daniel entered the fifth tent in the fourth row and walked to the third cot. "Isaac! Isaac, can you hear me?" he gently shook his sleeping brother.

Isaac slowly opened his eyes and looked around in a daze. "Where am I?" he whispered.

"Isaac, it is me, Danny. You are in a hospital."

"Did they shoot you too?"

"Isaac, I am your brother, Danny. I have come to take you home."

"Home? Is Lydia here?"

"No, Lydia is home in Fryeburg. You are in the hospital in Gettysburg. As soon as you are well enough, I will take you home to Lydia."

"I cannot walk. I lost my leg."

"We will not walk home. We will take a train."

"Darian saved me. I would have died if I was left out on that field. So many died. Where is he?"

"I suppose he left with the army to fight in the next battle. But he wrote us a letter before he left Gettysburg to tell me to find you and take you home."

"How can I tell Lydia that I lost my leg?"

"She already knows. Darian's letter told us."

"Tell her I am sorry."

"Tell her yourself. I will bring you some paper and a pen. But first you need to bathe and to put on clean clothes. Mama sent you soap and tea. Lydia packed some clean clothing for you. I have a sack with supplies back in the Christian Commission's tent. I will be right back."

Isaac grabbed his brother's arm. "Danny, are you really here? You came?"

"Yes, it is really me and I came to take you home." He swallowed the lump in his throat. "I have been searching for you for weeks and I found you."

"If you leave, do you promise to come back?"

"I promise to be back in ten minutes with a bag of items from home."

It took three basins' worth of water, two rags, one towel and a half of bar of soap to wash off a month's worth of filth from battle and neglect. "Now put on this clean shirt. Do you need help with your pants?"

"Danny, I am not three years old." He tried to balance on one leg. "Perhaps a little help, but Eli never hears about this."

"Never," Daniel solemnly promised with a grin.

"You brought my church shoes," Isaac complained.

"Lydia packed your clothes, not me." He knelt to tie the right shoe. "The letter did not mention which leg was amputated so she packed both," he explained after returning the left shoe to the canvas bag.

"Excuse me, sir," the soldier in the next cot called. "Please forgive my boldness. I lost my right leg, and if your brother does not need it, I would be most grateful to have the left shoe."

"Of course. I am…"

"You are Danny, and this is your brother Isaac and you came to take him home. There is no privacy here."

Danny laughed. He surveyed the unkempt, dirty soldier dressed in tatters. "My church shipped a crate of clothing to the Christian Commission warehouse. I will return with some clothes for you. They will not be fancy, but at least they will be clean."

Daniel returned with three nurses carrying wash basins and placed the clothing on the soldier's cot. "First we bathe," the oldest nurse informed, then we dress."

"Now, do you feel better?" she asked the newly washed patient wearing clean clothes.

"Oh yes, mam. I feel like a human being again. I am mighty grateful."

A tall, husky officer burst into the tent and demanded, "Ladies, what is the meaning of this?"

"I am simply caring for my patient. A clean body and clean clothing will help on his road to recovery."

"He is a prisoner of war. Half of these men are Confederates who were left behind. Under no circumstances whatsoever will citizens' clothing be carried into any of the hospitals.[3] I am tired of southern sympathizers secretly bringing in civilian clothing so these men can escape unnoticed."

"Young man," the petite, older lady wagged her finger at him, "First, no one shall question my loyalty to the Union. I have three grandsons fighting in this war. Secondly, there are no Union or Confederates in the eyes of our Lord Jesus Christ. These are all wounded soldiers who need our love and care. And lastly, if you have a clean Confederate uniform, I shall be happy to dress him in it. If not, then stand out of my way and let me do my job."

"I will report this to my supervisor."

"Sir?" Daniel interrupted. "If you are so concerned about prisoners escaping, why are you mixing the Confederates with Union troops? Would it not be easier to watch the prisoners, if they were separated?"

The officer's face turned red and he marched out of the tent.

Isaac laughed, "Danny, you would not make a very good soldier. No one questions an officer!"

The nurse addressed the patients in the tent. "Gentleman, we have two hours to get washed and dressed before dinner."

"Isaac, I brought paper, pen and ink. I think the family would prefer to receive letters from you instead of me. I can take them to the post office."

Dear Lydia,

Please forgive me for leaving you and the girls. All I thought about after the battle was coming home to you. I promised God if he would let me live, I would be a better husband and father. Danny found me here at a new army hospital. As soon as the doctors discharge me, I will come home, and I promise I will never leave again.

Your devoted husband,
Isaac

He sealed the letter and handed it to Daniel. "When can I go home?"

"That is not up to me. It is up to the doctors. The sooner you start eating and get your strength back, the sooner you will be able to go home."

Two weeks later, the brothers stood at the train station with Isaac carefully balanced on homemade wooden crutches and Daniel holding a dirty, empty canvas bag. Isaac anxiously boarded the train with some assistance. Daniel took one last look at Camp Letterman and waved goodbye to his friends in the U.S. Christian Commission before slowly entering the train and taking a seat beside his brother.

XII

The Return

Rachel nervously paced in front of the Oxford Hotel as she watched the stagecoach carrying her brothers, approach. She opened the door as the vehicle came to a stop. An exhausted Daniel stepped out and then reached in to help Isaac.

"Welcome home!" She tried to conceal her shock at the sight of her weak, emaciated brother.

Isaac, ignoring his sister, expectantly looked down the road searching for his family.

"Mama thought it would be best for the family to be reunited in private. They are all waiting for you at your house. Can you make it that far?" she asked.

Isaac did not want her pity. He took his crutches from the stagecoach and headed toward home. Daniel grabbed the canvas bag and silently followed.

"They are coming!" Emily excitedly reported as she looked out the front window.

Jacob hurried down the front stairs and headed up the street. "Welcome home, son!" Jacob embraced Isaac, "Your mother has been cooking for three days."

"Four days," Rachel corrected with a laugh.

Daniel and Rachel helped Isaac navigate the front steps as the front door flew open. "Isaac!" Kate gasped at the sight of her son.

"Hello, Mama. Do you have something good to eat?" he tried to smile.

"Danny, welcome home. I have missed you!" Emily greeted her husband with a warm embrace.

Isaac looked around and spotted his wife in the dining room staring at him "Lydia, I promised you I would come home." He could not bear the look of disappointment in her eyes.

"Summer, look at what a big girl you are!" he exclaimed for he still imagined them the same as the day he left.

"I am not Summer. I am Mahayla. Who are you?" she eyed her father suspiciously.

"I am your papa."

"What happened to your leg?" she pointed to the half empty pant leg.

"I lost it in the war."

"Well, I think you should go back and find it. Nana, can we eat now?"

"That is the best idea I have heard all day," Isaac smiled at his daughter. "I have not had a decent meal since I left home."

"Well, you must be very hungry," she replied earnestly.

"Would you do me the honor of sitting next to me, so we may become better acquainted?"

She looked to her mother before answering. "I always sit next to Uncle Danny," she protested.

"I will sit on one side of you and your papa will sit on the other," Daniel offered. "We cannot eat without your sister. Is she upstairs playing with her dolls? Could you please ask her to come down and join us?"

"Emily made the girls a family of dolls," Lydia explained. "Summer spends hours playing with them."

"I have never seen a child with such a vivid imagination!" Kate continued with pride. "She can entertain herself for hours, unlike someone else I know who is always into mischief."

"Please get your sister. You must learn to do as you are told," Lydia scolded.

She stood at the bottom of the back staircase and yelled, "Time to eat! Bring the dolls to show Papa. Uncle Danny is home!"

Lydia sighed in exasperation as Isaac suppressed a chuckle.

A little red headed girl with an armful of dolls ran down the stairs. "Uncle Danny, you came back to me!" she exclaimed excitedly.

"Yes, I did," he laughed as he picked up his niece. "And I brought your papa back to you too."

"Summer, would you like to show me your beautiful dolls?" Isaac invited as he patted the empty the empty chair beside him.

She cautiously approached her father. "This is Papa," she handed him a rag doll dressed in a blue uniform and cap.

"Where is your uniform?" Mahayla asked suspiciously. She was not yet convinced this one-legged stranger in brown pants and white shirt was her papa.

"It got dirty, so I left it at the hospital."

"This is Mama," Summer handed him a doll with auburn colored yarn for hair dressed in a green silk dress.

"She is beautiful just like your mama," Isaac approved.

"Aunt Emily gave us a bag of scraps to make doll clothes and quilts," Summer explained. She is teaching me to sew. My dolls will have the prettiest dresses in the world."

"I am sure they will. This doll must be Summer," he held up the small doll with red hair dressed in a white dress with little red flowers. "This must be Mahayla," he held the doll dressed in a rose-colored print dress and apron with brown wool roving braided in two pigtails. "Summer, you look just like your mama and Mahayla, you look like Aunt Rachel."

"I do not! Aunt Rachel is an old lady!" she replied indignantly.

"Mahayla, go to your room this minute!" Lydia demanded.

When Isaac stopped laughing, he contradicted, "Lydia, she is fine. Do you know that Aunt Rachel is my big sister?"

"She is?" Mahayla looked at her aunt.

"She is the best big sister anyone could ask for. When I was little, Aunt Rachel, Uncle Eli and Uncle Danny were already grownups. I was always underfoot and getting into trouble."

"You got into trouble too?" She asked with new interest.

"Always," Rachel confirmed.

"Aunt Rachel and my grandparents helped me grow up just like Uncle Danny and Aunt Emily help you grow up."

"Your grandparents are dead you know."

"I know. They lived in this house and I spent a lot of time visiting them. I miss them very much."

"Just like I visit Grandpa and Nana at the farm?"

"Just like," Isaac nodded.

Summer silently listened as her sister crossed her arms and declared, "I think I might like you."

"I hope so. I certainly like you! And Summer. I like Uncle Danny and Aunt Emily and I am very thankful that they were here to help take care of you while I was away. But your papa is home now to take care of you. It is time for Uncle Danny and Aunt Emily to return to their house at the lumber mill.

They can visit whenever they want, and Aunt Emily will still teach you to sew doll clothes," he quickly added as he saw Summer's lower lip quiver.

"How am I supposed to run this house, watch the girls and now take care of you by myself? Can you chop wood and fill the wood boxes? Can you carry the girls upstairs to bed every night? Can you…" she burst into tears and ran upstairs.

"Your mama is having one of her spells," Emily quietly explained.

"When we are done eating this delicious meal, I will take the girls back to the store for a visit. We can look through my bag of fabric scraps and I may find a peppermint drop or two," Rachel invited. "We will let the grownups have grownup talk. You can play with your dolls. Uncle Peter might have some scraps of wood. Perhaps your papa can build a doll bed."

"You do not need two legs to build a doll bed," Mahayla explained to her father.

"I do not," Isaac agreed. "Now let us enjoy this meal that Nana made for us."

"Aunt Emily and I helped," Summer added.

"You can sew and cook? You are becoming quite the young lady."

"Mahayla helps me in my herb garden, just like you did when you were a boy," Kate added. "Our food is getting cold," she reminded. The family finished their meal in awkward silence.

After dishes were washed and put away, Rachel took the girls and their dolls. "I will have them back at bedtime," she promised. She hugged Isaac as she whispered, "They need some time."

Kate made a pot of chamomile tea and Emily brought Lydia downstairs. The family gathered around the kitchen table. Jacob cleared his throat. "We will never understand the deprivations, the hardships and dare I say the horrors our soldiers have endured these past few years. They are not the same carefree boys who left for war.

Isaac, you will never fully understand the deprivations, the hardships and the strain of worry the family has endured. We are not the same family you left behind. Eli and Julia are worried sick that they have heard nothing from David since Gettysburg."

"David is missing?"

"Yes. And we have not received any word from Darian since his letter telling us you were wounded," Jacob continued.

"Danny, why did you not tell me!" Isaac demanded.

"I wanted you to focus on getting better and getting home. I hoped by the time we returned to Fryeburg, Emily would have received a letter." His voice cracked with emotion.

"We are not the only family dealing with this horrible war. Mrs. Quint is still reeling from the loss of her son."

"Monroe is dead?" Isaac shook his head.

"Yes, and there are many families who have buried their sons, husbands, brothers and fathers. We must extend our help and comfort to them even amid our own struggles.

Lydia," he turned to his daughter-in-law, "You have much to be thankful. There are many widows caring for young children who have lost their homes and do not have family to take them in."

"God created families to care for one another. One generation helps raise the children while another cares for the elderly," Kate stated.

"Lydia's mother is gone. I could never take her mother's place, but Lydia is the daughter I never had. The girls are the grandchildren I never had," Emily explained to Isaac.

"This will be an adjustment for all of you. Lydia needs Emily's help. Danny and Emily are family to the girls. Until they know you better," Jacob began.

"Do I not have any say in my own home!" Isaac demanded.

"A father provides what is best for his family. It is best to have Emily and Danny stay a little longer. The day will soon come when the family has adjusted and will no longer need the extra help".

"Be grateful that you are alive. Gettysburg is filled with graves," Daniel reminded. "Be grateful you only lost one leg. What would you do if you lost your right arm? Or your mind like many poor souls we have witnessed?"

Lydia silently drank her tea as she pondered the words of her in-laws.

Isaac was suddenly overwhelmed with fatigue. "What you say makes sense. It will take time for me to get my strength back," he admitted. "I will be most grateful for your help, Danny. It has been an exhausting journey and a long day. I need to rest." He grabbed his crutches and headed to the back stairs.

"Your bedroom is downstairs," Lydia instructed.

"Why?"

"We feared that you would be unable to manage the stairs by yourself. It is only temporary," Emily quickly added. "The girls and I made a new quilt for your bed and Eli helped us move furniture. Let me show you," she offered cheerfully.

They approached his grandfather's law office. "But this office has always been locked," Isaac protested.

"I think Grandpa would be very proud and happy to share his office with you," Danny explained.

"Where is Grandpa's conference table?" Isaac asked.

"I sold it to Attorney Hastings" Lydia answered.

"But why?" he demanded.

"Because he needed a table and I needed the money! The girls were sick, and I had to pay the doctor. Your measly soldier's salary never covered all our expenses. Millers never accept charity. Is that not what you told me?"

"But that table belonged to my grandfather," he protested.

"Well, he is not using it, is he now!" she snapped, left the room and ran upstairs.

"She needs time, son," Jacob reassured.

Emily changed the subject. "Summer helped select the fabric for the quilt. Eli brought the bed, dresser and washstand over from the farm. And he took an old chair and made a commode."

Isaac blushed in humiliation.

"It is only temporary," Emily assured.

"Excuse me, but I need to rest," he stared at the family until they left the room, shutting the double doors behind them. He stared at the windows in dismay. He grabbed his crutches and closed the drapes while he awkwardly balanced on one leg. He was not going to allow curious neighbors peeking in to watch the sleeping invalid!

Exhausted, he pulled back the cotton sheets and quilt and collapsed into bed fully dressed. The comfort of the mattress newly filled with clean, dry corn husks, the scent of clean linens and the softness of the feather pillow enveloped him as he drifted off into a fitful sleep.

The creaking of the opening door woke him hours later. "Lydia?" he called hopefully in the darkness.

"Papa, it is me." As Mahayla opened the door wide, some of the light in the foyer streamed in. "I thought you might be lonely, so I brought you this." She handed him the Mahayla doll. "We sleep in Mama's bed, so she does not get lonely."

He propped himself up on one elbow and took the doll. "Thank you, Mahayla. You are very thoughtful."

"I asked Aunt Rachel how you lost your leg. She said I ask too many questions. How did you lose your leg?" she asked boldly as she sat at the edge of the bed.

"In war soldiers shoot at each other."

"That does not sound safe to me."

"You are absolutely right. One bullet hit me in the leg."

"Did you see the doctor? The doctor came to our house when I got sick."

"Yes. He said it was never going to get better."

"Did he give you medicine?"

"He gave me medicine, so it would not hurt too much, but he did not have medicine to make my leg better. He said if I wanted to live and go home to my little girls, he had to cut it off."

"Did it hurt?"

"No. I was asleep. But it hurt when I woke up."

Her eyes widened in horror. "Will it grow back? When Aunt Emily cuts my hair, it grows back."

"No. It will not grow back."

"I am going to pray that God grows it back."

"Mahayla, I have been looking for you!" Lydia entered the room holding a lantern. "It is past your bedtime."

"Mama, is a doctor going to cut off my leg when I go to sleep tonight?" she asked fearfully.

"Isaac, how dare you scare my daughter with your war stories! How dare you!" She grabbed Mahayla's hand and slammed the door behind her.

"What a day!" he thought bitterly. He stared into the darkness but could not fall asleep.

XIII

A Long Row to Hoe

It was a brisk September morning and the first of the leaves were beginning to turn yellow. "Emily, the ham and eggs are delicious," Isaac complimented.

"It is good to see that your appetite has finally returned. But Lydia cooked the breakfast. She is becoming quite a good cook," Emily smiled at her student.

"Thank you, Lydia. The house looks real nice too."

"Aunt Emily and Mama are making a new dress for the first day of school," Summer added.

"You are going to school next week?"

"Papa, I am six years old. I went to school last year."

"I am not going," Mahayla crossed her arms against her chest.

Isaac looked at his wife questioningly.

"Your mother and I discussed it. We feel she needs another year to mature and settle down. She helps your mother in the garden, practices penmanship on your old slate and I read aloud to her."

"It sounds like you made a very wise decision."

"Girls, your papa has a big day today. He is going to ride his horse to the farm and help Grandpa with chores," Daniel announced. "Not all day, of course. Just a few hours in the morning to start. Let me show you the steps I built for you to climb on the horse. Pa made a duplicate set for the farm. I made a leather sling which ties to the saddle horn to hold your crutches."

Isaac looked doubtful. Mahayla clapped her hands. "Papa, can you give me a ride, so I can help Nana pick her plants. Mama will not allow me to walk there by myself."

"You listen to your, Mama. Lydia, what do you think of me giving her a ride?"

"I think that sounds like a wonderful idea." She smiled at the thought of having a quiet morning without her spirited daughter.

With a little assistance from Daniel, he managed to get up in the saddle and place his crutches in the sling. Daniel handed Mahayla to him and they slowly left the yard.

"I never rode a horse before! Faster, Papa, faster."

"Maybe tomorrow." They made the short ride without mishap and entered the farmyard. Jacob grabbed the wooden steps and placed it by the horse. As Isaac swung his stump over the horse and slid down, he missed the step and fell to the ground.

Eli put his hand out to help me up. "I can do this!" Isaac snapped. With all his concentration and upper body strength, he got on his knees. Putting his hand on the step stool he pushed himself up on one leg, while holding onto the horse for balance. He grabbed his crutches and hobbled away.

"Papa. Don't forget me!" she put out her arms.

"I have you," Eli grabbed her and put her down.

Isaac silently resented his brother's interference.

"We need to pick the beans and corn today. My old knees are telling me we will have a frost soon."

"Grandpa, your knees cannot talk!" she giggled.

"It is just an expression," Jacob explained. "Now run in the kitchen and surprise your grandmother."

Eli handed his brother a scythe. "How is this going to work?" he asked doubtfully.

"He could drive the wagon, while we cut the corn stalks and throw them in," Jacob suggested.

Eli helped his brother get into the wagon. "You are nothing but skin and bones."

"Give your mother a few months and she will fatten him up," Jacob predicted.

The trio had worked slowly for two hours when Jacob held unto a corn stalk and closed his eyes. "Pa!" Eli went running over to him.

Jacob patted his eldest son on the shoulder. "Nothing to worry about. Just one of my little spells."

"Your little spells are coming more frequently. Let me help you in the wagon and get you in the house. You should not be doing this work, he is," Eli glared at Isaac.

"Pa, what spells?"

"Isaac, it is nothing to worry about. I just over did it and got tired. A cup of oat straw tea with a biscuit and I will be back at work."

"A cup of tea, a biscuit and a rest," Eli corrected as he assisted his father and carefully placed him in the wagon on top of the corn stalks.

"What would I do without you, son."

"Pa, what would we do without each other. Close your eyes and rest." Eli hopped in the front, grabbed the reins from Isaac and slowly drove to the barn. "Unhitch the horse while I help Pa in the house," he instructed. Isaac watched his brother help his father enter the house.

Isaac surveyed the situation. He leaned his crutches on the side of the wagon. He gingerly got down from the wagon and leaned against the horse for balance. Putting his arms around the animal's neck he whispered, "I will never let you go to war. Never!" He tried to block out the shrieks of wounded horses and the sight of rotting animal carcasses from his mind.

"Just be patient with me girl," he patted the animal on her head. He slowly but successfully unhitched the wagon and the horse walked itself into the stall. She looked at Isaac expectantly.

As he studied the stack of hay against the outside wall, he realized he needed both arms to carry the hay. He leaned his crutches against the stall, hopped on one leg, gathered up a large armful of hay and hopped back to the stall. Losing his balance, he fell into the stall dropping the hay.

The horse snorted, backed up, put her head near Isaac's and nudged him. Isaac put his arms around the horse's neck and allowed the animal to lift her head and bring Isaac to a stand. Isaac laughed. "Good girl!"

Grabbing his crutches, he slowly hobbled to the house and carefully made his way up the front stairs.

"Pa, he is useless." Isaac overheard through the opened window.

"Eli, your brother has a long row to hoe. He needs our patience and understanding. I am just grateful to have my son back home. I do not care if he is missing a leg. He is alive and home."

"The problem is, we have crops to harvest and the two of us cannot do it ourselves."

"We did it last year."

"Just barely. Last year you were not having so many of your spells."

Isaac entered the kitchen. "Pa, why did you not tell me about this?"

"I did not wish to worry you. Besides what could you do about it being so far from home?"

"I am sure there are plenty of things you did not write about to us," Eli accused. "Where is my son? We have not heard from him in two months! What are you not telling us?"

"I have not seen David since the first day of the battle. There are only five explanations for not hearing from him."

"Such as?"

"He survived the battle and moved on with the army. With no writing supplies, he is unable to write home. He was captured by the enemy and he is sitting in a prisoner of war camp. He is still in Gettysburg injured and unidentified. Or he was killed in battle and buried. I have seen men hit by an artillery shell and blown to bits. There is no way you could identify the body."

"You said five reasons," Eli reminded.

"Or he deserted."

"I did not raise my son to be a coward!" he yelled pounding his fist on the table.

"Hundreds of men, no thousands of good men have deserted. Everyone has their breaking point."

"Pa, you rest. I need to get back to work." Eli stood up and hurriedly left.

"Son, I am so sorry for what you have gone through," he patted Isaac on the hand. "Perhaps it would be best if we both got some rest. Your brother is worried about David. I understand the feeling. Can you get back on the horse yourself?"

"Yes, Pa." It was easier mounting the horse the second time. As he rode home, he had an idea. He rode past his house, past the general store where Rachel laughed and waved to him through the window and past the Oxford Hotel where passengers were climbing down from a stagecoach. For the first time in months, he felt free to travel where he wanted without depending on someone for help. He stopped at the new brick Fryeburg Academy where he carefully slid off the horse, grabbed his crutches and slowly made his way up the granite steps.

"Isaac Miller, it is wonderful to see you looking so well. All of you boys have been in our prayers. It is a shame about Monroe Quint," the secretary shook her head. "How may I help you today?"

"I need to see Headmaster Snow."

"Do you have an appointment? Mr. Snow is extremely busy with school starting in another week."

An office door quickly opened. "No Miller needs an appointment to see me!" the headmaster heartily greeted. Fryeburg Academy had closed for the 1861-62 school year because of the impact of the war. School resumed in the fall of 1862 under the leadership of Benjamin P. Snow, a graduate of Bowdoin College.[1] Although Mr. Snow did not personally know Isaac, he knew that Senator Benjamin Miller, one of the Academy's trustees, played a crucial role in rebuilding the school after it burned to the ground a decade ago. "Come on in! How may I help you?"

"My father is not in the best of health and I am limited in my usefulness on the farm. We need help in harvesting and most of the able-bodied men are gone. Could you recruit as many students as possible to work on the farm before school opens? I will gladly pay them from my government pension."

"Let me see what I can do. It is wonderful to have you back home. These are terrible times," he shook his head. "So many of our boys off to war. Let us hope that is bloody war ends soon. Thank you for stopping by."

Isaac discovered it was more difficult descending the steps than it was to ascend. How to mount the horse without his wooden stool? Reverend David Sewall walked by. "Isaac, it is wonderful to see you out and about! Does this mean I will see you in church this Sunday?"

"If you can help me up on this horse, I promise I will be in church," he bartered.

"That sounds like a fair deal to me!"

The next morning, Isaac eagerly mounted the horse using the stool and rode to the farm. Four boys ranging in age from thirteen to fifteen arrived that morning to help. The next morning seven boys worked. By the end of the week they had nine boys who nearly completed the harvest.

"All we have left are the root vegetables," Jacob stated with satisfaction. "We can take our time getting those in. Thank you, Isaac. I should have thought of this myself."

"I can hire a few boys to stack the firewood after school," Isaac offered.

"I can stack firewood," Eli grumbled.

"So, you can. I need to return home and hear about Summer's first day of school."

With a new confidence, he mounted his horse and galloped home.

* * *

Isaac kept his promise to Reverend Sewall. With encouragement from Mahayla and a firm arm hold by Daniel, he safely navigated the granite steps and slowly walked down the aisle of the Congregational Church. He was surprised to see the sanctuary half empty, with sons, fathers, husbands and brothers missing. Mr. and Mrs. Quint sadly sat together in a back pew and there was an empty space beside Eli and Julia. Although everything looked the same as he remembered, nothing felt the same. And it never would.

* * *

It was the beginning of October and no one heard from Darian or David in three months. Isaac found Eli doing chores in the barn. "Where is Pa?"

"He is resting."

"I fear the strain of this war is wearing on him." Isaac commented. "Emily and Danny are trusting the Lord to watch over Darian. Danny says, that is all they can do."

"Enough talk. Feed the animals while I dig the potatoes. Unless you hired someone to do that for you too."

Isaac bit his tongue. He had watched his brother quickly descend deeper into helpless anger. He turned to scoop out some grain when he lost his balance and fell to the floor smashing his face against the wall. He let out a stream of curses as he wiped the blood from his nose.

"Stop complaining! You had your life handed to you on a silver platter. You never worked for or built your own house. You inherited the biggest house in town. You have never done a day's work in your life! Now you come home thinking you are a hero! I would give anything to have you dead and my son home instead!"

Isaac smashed Eli's face with his crutch. In a rage Eli grabbed Isaac by the shirt collar and slammed him against the wall.

Jacob came running in the barn. "Boys! Boys! Stop it! Eli, you know better than to…"

"Beat up a cripple!" Eli finished the sentence and dropped Isaac to the ground.

Jacob covered his face with both hands and began to sob, "Oh Lord, forgive me for forgetting you during the decades of my prosperity. I thought my hard work alone brought my success. Lord I am losing my family before my very eyes. My two grandsons are missing. I am in despair."

"Pa, I am sorry. I lost my temper. Let me help you inside. Mama will make you some chamomile tea."

"Help your brother up first," he commanded.

"I neither want nor need his help!" Isaac snapped as he gathered his crutches and painfully stood up.

"Eli, wait for me here. We need to talk. Isaac, come with me." The brothers obeyed.

"Mercy, what happened to you?" Kate asked Isaac as she poured the two men their tea.

"I fell and smashed my face against the wall."

"Let me get some salve for those scrapes. We do not wish for them to become infected."

"I am sorry, Papa. I lost my temper when Eli said that he wished I was dead, and David was home."

"Jacob, you must talk to that boy," Kate admonished. "He is getting out of hand. We are all worried sick about David and Darian. All I can think of is poor Mrs. Quint grieving the loss of Monroe. I fear we will receive a letter from …"

"It is not worth it. This war is not worth the price we are paying. We should have let the South leave. Who needs them?" Isaac declared bitterly. "I lost my leg. I cannot work to support my family. For what?"

"Come with me to the front parlor. Kate, will you please excuse us?"

"Certainly, I am on my way to the general store. I shall be back in an hour." She grabbed her bonnet and briskly walked up the road.

"Have a seat," Jacob directed as he grabbed some papers from Aunt Grace's oak writing desk. "I am about to break a promise I had made to my father over fifty years ago. I am going to reveal a family secret. You must promise to never tell anyone."

"Pa, I do not understand." Isaac began reading the papers handed to him.

> *I, Benjamin James Miller in the town of Fryeburg of the Province of Maine, in the Commonwealth of*

Massachusetts hereby grant complete freedom to the slave, Hannah Chase, formerly known as Royal Randolph who was purchased by me from Mr. and Mrs. Henry Chase of Philadelphia on August 1, 1792, intending to convey any and all rights of a free person of these United States of America.

Benjamin James Miller, Esquire
April 2, 1793

"I do not understand," Isaac stammered. "Grandpa bought a slave?"

"Yes, and that slave was your grandmother. He had to buy her, so he could legally move her from Philadelphia to here. Then he granted her freedom and they married."

"Why was Nana a slave?"

"One great grandfather was an African brought to America in a slave ship. A series of mixed-race mothers and white masters led to a very light skinned slave. If it was not for the love of your grandfather who granted her freedom, all of us could have been born slaves."

"That is impossible."

"Not only is it possible, it is true. We have kin who are slaves in Virginia and possibly throughout the south. If we win this war, there will be no more slavery. Our relatives will be free like us. That is what you fought for. That is what you lost your leg for. It is better to be a free man with one leg than a slave with two."

"Why did Grandpa not tell us?"

"Marrying a slave is illegal. If he had revealed the truth, he could have been disbarred or jailed. What do you think would happen to your grandmother?"

"Why did he keep the letter, so people could find it?"

"It was safely locked in his desk. I believed he may have kept it in case any slave catchers asked questions, they would have proof of her purchase and redemption. He may have died before he had the opportunity to destroy it. I found it when I was cleaning out his desk.

I could not bring myself to destroy it. But now I realize I must." He opened the door to the wood stove and threw the document in.

"Does Eli know?"

"No one knows, not even your mother. I want you to realize that you fought for something much bigger than yourself, much bigger than this family. Do you understand what is at stake? Sure, the family managed to smuggle slaves to Canada and to freedom. This war could free all the slaves with a stroke of a pen."

"This family has broken the law for three generations," Isaac observed.

"Four," Jacob corrected. "My grandfather, James Miller, consented to what he referred to as God's calling."

"Danny has continued God's calling at the mill. He could go to jail if he is caught." Isaac knew about Daniel's activities since he was a boy. Today he fully realized the high price that his brother was willing to pay for his convictions.

"He could have. But the Emancipation Proclamation has changed that now. Live your life proudly as a free man. Make your grandfather proud of you. The Lord has a plan for you. I suspect it is not farming. Go home to your family."

Jacob sat in his chair deep in thought. He had to choose his words wisely. He slowly headed to the field where Eli was digging potatoes.

"Elijah!" Jacob called. "Meet me in the house."

Eli came running. "Are you feeling poorly?"

"No. I am fine. I wish to speak to you."

"And Isaac?"

"I sent him home." The two men walked silently into the kitchen and sat down.

"I have failed as a father."

"Pa! How can you say such a thing?"

Jacob put his hand up to silence him. "You know that I am not a learned man. I barely finished grammar school. I left the teaching to the teachers and the preaching to the preachers. It was your mother who raised all of you. Your grandmother was the role model of a Godly Christian, not me. I was too busy farming."

"But Pa, you taught me everything I know about farming! Look how much this farm has grown since you took it over from Uncle Micah."

"There is more to life than farming. I had forgotten that. There are more important things that I should have taught you."

"Such as?"

"You know your mother and I understand your fears about David. We feared for Isaac's life too. Would Danny find him? Would Isaac survive? What will happen to him when he comes home? Will he be able to work? I understand your pain. I have had many sleepless nights. Plus, I have two missing grandsons and two sons worried about them. There is nothing as a father I can do to make everything come out all right. I do not know the future. I have no strength left over to lend to you and Danny.

I failed to teach you about your heavenly Father. He is the only one in charge of this situation. I have failed to teach you to depend on Him and not on ourselves."

"The day my son returns safely home, will be the day that I believe that there is a heavenly Father in control of the events in my life."

Jacob sighed. "Do you remember the parable Jesus told about the Prodigal Son?"

"Yes, sir."

"Good. Tell it to me. I do not think I could find it in the Bible."

"There once was a man who had two sons. The younger son asked for his inheritance in advance and the father gave it to him. The son took off and squandered the father's hard earn money…"

"I do not remember the Bible saying hard earned. But continue."

"He squandered the money on sinful living until he had no more money or friends and found himself eating with the pigs. I thought Jewish people did not keep pigs."

"Maybe the son was working for a Gentile farmer."

"I wonder what breeds of pigs they had in Israel back then?"

Jacob shook his head and laughed. "Clearly I raised a farmer and not a preacher! What did the son say to himself?"

"Even the servants in my father's house eat better than this. Maybe if I go home my father will hire me as one of his servants. One day the father sees the younger son in the distance returning home."

"I bet that father scanned the horizon everyday hoping his son would return. Just the way you look up the road every afternoon hoping to see David coming home.

The point of the story is the father was hoping and looking for his lost son. Now the two of us can relate to that. The father is so excited to have his son back, he wants to throw a big party and invite all his friends. And the older brother was just as excited to see him, right?"

"Well, not really. I mean why should he be? The younger brother left the family, foolishly wasted all his money and the father wants to throw him a party! What about the older brother? He was the hard working, loyal one. Did his father ever throw him a party?"

"I think I remember the father said everything I own here is yours. You could kill a fattened calf and have your party whenever you wanted. But my son was lost and now is found. Your grandmother would have done a much better job retelling this."

"No, Aunt Grace would have done a much better job. She would have described the menu, the robes and jewelry people were wearing," Eli laughed.

"I miss those two dear ladies and my father. Do not deny me the joy of having my son return home to me. I can love one son and still miss my two grandsons."

"Now, I do not remember. Did the older brother go to the party?"

"The Bible does not say. The question is, would you?" Jacob challenged.

"I have potatoes to dig."

* * *

It was time for the Fryeburg Fair. Normally Eli and the rest of the town would be filled with excitement. Six years ago, Eli was instrumental in purchasing the seven-acre parcel just a half mile from the village. He took pride in the newly built Agricultural Building.[2]

He glumly walked down Elm Street. It would not be the same this year without David. The war impacted many aspects of Fryeburg life, including the fair. Attendance was down last year; this year fewer farmers were participating. In the livestock division there were only three entries for cows and one flock of sheep.[3] With many local tanneries, leather exhibits were always popular. This year only one tannery responded to participate.[4]

Thanks to Rachel's exhortations, ladies became associate members in 1860. Now the fair offered premiums for needlework, honey, syrups, wines, jellies and preserves.[5] Today he was grateful for that decision because many of the entries were submitted by women. Most of the attendees would be older men, women and children because most of the younger men were off to war.

Maybe next year the war will be over and Fryeburg, the fair and his family will go back to normal. Maybe next year.

* * *

"Mama! Mama!" Summer shrieked.

"Mercy! What is wrong!" Lydia picked up her skirts and ran up the stairs into the spare the bedroom where Summer was sobbing.

"Look! Look what she did!" Summer held up Papa doll with its left leg cut off at the knee.

Mahayla sat on the floor holding a pair of scissors. "Papa doll lost his leg in the war," she calmly explained. "It's my Papa doll, not yours!" she grabbed the doll from her sister.

"Mahayla, give me those scissors. You know better than to take Aunt Emily's scissors without permission.

"Mama, it's ruined forever!" Summer cried.

"Ruined forever," Lydia thought as she choked back tears.

XIV

A New Beginning

"Rachel, I need your help in ordering a special item," Kate greeted her daughter as she entered the store.

"Of course, Mama. What is it?"

"I need to buy a wooden leg for Isaac. He will never be able to work with one leg. He needs to be away from Eli and have his own business."

"Come to the back room with me and we will look at some catalogs." The two women sat silently turning page after page. "Here it is! I knew I saw this advertisement somewhere!"

> *Marks' Artificial Limbs*
> *A.A. Marks, 701 Broadway, New York City*
>
> *The improved rubber hand and foot possess the quality yielding to every essential angle of the natural, without the use of complicated hinges, joints and contrivances which annoy and render expensive their daily use.*[1]

"Look a photograph of a man who lost both legs in a railroad accident. One above the knee and one below the knee. He can walk half a mile in eight minutes without a cane. He can perform a day's work without unusual fatigue; can go up and down stairs. Look we can order one!" Kate exclaimed.

> *From our Illustrated Measuring Sheet, Artificial Limbs can be made and shipped to all parts of the world, without the presence of the patient, with guaranteed success. A manual of Artificial Limbs and Illustrated Measuring Sheets sent free upon application.*[2]

"This is the answer to my prayers."
"But, Mama, how will you afford it?"
"I am retiring from the butter making business and selling my cows."
"But, Mama, you have been making butter your whole life."
"Farming is changing. Dairy farmers are now selling their milk to creameries who then make butter on a much larger scale. I am tired of churning. I will enter the apothecary business full time selling my remedies all over Maine and New Hampshire."
"Papa will never allow you to travel the countryside alone."
"Of course not. Isaac will.

* * *

"Does it fit?" Kate asked anxiously through the closed door.
Isaac opened the double doors of his grandfather's office and walked out unsteadily. "It feels very strange," he admitted.
"Look at you!" Lydia gasped.
"I prayed your leg would grow back!" Mahayla squealed. "I knew it would happen. I just knew it!"
"Well, ladies, let us walk up to the farm. We have much work to do before I can go off and sell Miller's Remedies. When Danny comes home tonight, we will design our peddler wagon and order the lumber. Now that I can stand on my own two feet, I can begin to build it."

"I do not believe my eyes. Look who is walking up the road!" Jacob called to Eli who was busy cutting ears of corns off the stalks.

"Is it David? Has David come home?" Eli came running.

"No. It is Isaac walking on his new leg with Kate, Lydia and Mahayla."

"Oh," Eli returned to his labors.

"I fear I need to sit down. My leg is quite painful," Isaac admitted.

"Perhaps we were too ambitious. Let me put some calendula salve on the stump and bandage it. Let's go inside."

Kate grabbed a tin of salve from her pantry and applied it and a fresh bandage. She added some soft, carded wool as a cushion. "Perhaps you should wear it a few hours at a time until you have developed a callus. I will be right back." She left for the front parlor and returned with Benjamin Miller's ebony cane.

"I could never use Grandpa's cane. People will think I am putting on airs," Isaac protested.

"No, people will think you need to put some of your weight on a cane while you adjust to your new leg. Now stand up and try it," she instructed.

He took a few steps. "You are right. It does feel better. If you ladies do not need me, I will join Pa and Eli in the barn."

He gingerly walked into the barn. "Pa, can I help cutting ears off stalks?"

"We can surely use the help," Jacob smiled. "It will be like old times."

The three men worked silently. Eli did not mention Isaac's leg and Isaac had learned to simply avoid his brother to keep peace.

* * *

Over thirty people crowded into the Miller's barn on Saturday night for a husking bee. Neighbors, acquaintances, Mr. and Mrs. Quint and Reverend and Mrs. Seward enjoyed the food and fellowship.

"Mahayla, what do you have there?" Mrs. Quint asked.

"This is Papa Doll. He lost part of his leg fighting in the war. But Aunt Rachel got a new leg at the store. See?" she pointed to a stick tied around the half-empty, left leg. "And this is Mahayla Doll."

People smiled and nodded in approval. Someone brought out their fiddle. Neighbors gossiped, worked and laughed. For one evening everyone forgot about the war. Everyone but Eli.

* * *

"I did not know you could build things," Lydia admired.

"Pa taught me. When you are a farmer, you need to be a jack-of-all-trades." He showed her the diagram of a peddler's wagon he had drawn. "I am taking the old wagon from Grandpa's stable and making two doors on each side. Then I will enclose the back of the wagon and build two large trunks to sit on top."

"Now I understand. With the back fully enclosed, you will need the doors to reach inside."

I will build shelves and cabinets. I will have runners for winter and wheels for spring through fall. I plan to paint it black and in yellow lettering it will say Miller's Remedies."

"How about Miller's Traveling Apothecary?" Lydia suggested.

"I like that!"

* * *

Mahayla enjoyed the autumn sunshine as she picked flowers from Nana's herb garden. She dragged a half-bushel basket of bright orange flowers to the kitchen where Kate and Lydia were tying bundles of flowers to hang upside down in the attic to dry.

"Well, someone has been busy!" Kate complimented her granddaughter. "What are these flowers called?"

"Calendula. First, we dry them and then we make a salve. It is good for cuts and scrapes. Papa uses it on his hurt leg," Mahayla proudly explained. "These little white flowers are chamomile and they make my favorite tea."

Kate never explained that chamomile aids in digestion, relieves menstrual cramps and calms nerves.[3] She often served the tea to her high-strung granddaughter.

Lydia was stripping dried green leaves off their stems. "Nana, what herb is that? All the green leaves look alike to me."

"It is thyme. We are making a tea to settle an upset stomach or a cough."[4]

"I have trouble telling apart thyme from oregano."

"You can use oregano or thyme for an upset stomach or a cough too," Lydia explained.

Kate was proud of both of her pupils. Perhaps Miller's Traveling Apothecary would become her legacy. She showed Mahayla a large crock filled with dry comfrey. "Do you remember that this is for?"

"They grow wild like weeds all over the place. The flowers are pretty, but they are not medicine. You use the dry leaves to make medicine to put on cuts.[5] I thought you put yarrow on cuts?"

"Like comfrey you can put warm tea to clean a wound. You can drink yarrow tea, but you cannot drink comfrey tea. You only use it on the outside.[6] Different plants can do the same job. Now we will make calendula salve. Take these dried flowers and fill the crock to the top, while I heat the lard on the stove."

When both tasks were accomplished, Kate poured the warm liquid into the crock covering all the flowers. She carefully stirred all the air bubbles out of the mixture before tightly sealing the crock. "Now we will store it right here by the stove to stay warm for the next four to six weeks."

"Are we finished?"

"No, we are not. Now for the fun part." She placed another large crock onto the Liberty Table, grabbed an iron pot and covered the top with cheese cloth. She slowly poured the mixture through the cheese cloth and the flowers remained on top.

"You may help your mother chip small pieces of bees wax from the brick of wax." She skillfully added the bees wax into the calendula oil as it heated on the stove.

"How do you know when you have added enough wax?" Lydia asked.

"Experience." Kate handed Mahayla a willow basket. Please go to the pantry and you will find a crate filled with tins. Fill up the basket and bring the tins to me."

"What are they for?"

"To put the salve in so we can sell them to people. I am going to teach your mother how to do this. When you are a little older, I shall teach you." She placed a small balance scale on the table. "It is for weighing our salves," she anticipated her granddaughter's question. "First we weigh the tin. Then we will add four ounces of salve in the tin. It will harden as it cools."[7]

"Then we put it in Papa's new wagon and sell it."

"You have certainly learned a great deal in the past few weeks."

"Yes, I did. I do not have to go to boring school to learn things. You can teach me everything I need to know. I like this much better than making butter."

"So, do I," Kate agreed.

* * *

"It is almost November, when do you think the wagon will be finished? Snow will be coming soon," Lydia asked her husband.

"I am not concerned. I will put runners on it. Would you care to accompany me on my first trip to Portland? Emily can watch the girls."

"That sounds lovely. Your mother has taught me so much. I believe I could sell our remedies."

"We will have adventures together. This will be a new beginning for us," he smiled at his wife.

"I would like that." She linked her arm through his. "A new beginning."

* * *

Lydia set the dining room table with Isaac's grandmother's china.

"What is the occasion?" Isaac asked. "Look at this food! Ham, pie, potatoes."

"Please everyone, take a seat. Tonight, we are celebrating," Lydia explained.

As bowls and platters were passed Mahayla asked, "What are we celabating?"

"Family. I did not have real family growing up. At least not like this family. I know my mother did her best. I now know what it is like to be part of a family and to help each other. I learned how to care for my children and to be part of a business. Emily and Danny, I do not know how to thank you for all the sacrifices you have made for us these past two years."

"We are family," Emily smiled.

"I think we are now ready to be a family on our own. Danny should not have to travel back and forth to the mill for another winter. Emily, you have your own home."

Mahayla started to cry. "You are leaving us?"

"They can visit us," Summer consoled her sister. "We can visit them."

"Of course," Emily agreed. "Also, I will stay with you when your mother accompanies your father on business trips. It will be a new beginning for all of us."

XV

Discovery in Gettysburg

Gettysburg, November 18, 1863

Reporter, Thaddeus Pierce, had sworn he would never return to Gettysburg. Yet here he was with suitcase in hand stepping down from a crowded train into the Gettysburg train depot. His editor had sent him to cover the dedication of the Soldiers National Cemetery.

When Pennsylvania Governor, Andrew Curtain, had visited the town days after the battle, he was appalled at the sight of animals digging up the remains of soldiers who had been hastily buried in shallow graves. He wanted the Union soldiers to receive a proper and dignified burial. With the assistance of attorney David Wills, they petitioned the federal government to establish a proper cemetery.[1]

Soldiers National Cemetery was fittingly established on Cemetery Hill, part of the battlefield. Thousands of the battle dead were exhumed from shallow graves, identified and separated from the bodies of Confederates. The fallen soldiers were buried in semicircular rows in state plots. Although reinternments had begun early in the fall, the burials had not yet been completed.[2] Two days before, the remains of Private Monroe Quint were placed in a coffin and buried in the Maine State Section Row D, Section 11.

Pierce's thoughts were not on the cemetery, but on arriving at the Wagon Hotel in time to reserve a room, eat a decent meal and have a drink. As he briskly walked down Baltimore Street, he thankfully noted that the stench of four months ago had dissipated.

"I will have a scotch," he ordered as he wearily placed his suitcase down by the front desk, "and a room please. In that order."

The hotel keeper laughed. "Are you here for tomorrow's dedication? I understand that Edward Everett will be making quite a speech."

"Yes, I know. The New York Post sent me to cover the story."

Not to be out done, the hotel keeper added, "Did you know that President Lincoln is arriving tonight by a special train and staying at the home of David Wills?"

"Really?"

"Wills invited the President to make a few concluding remarks after Everett's oration."[3]

"Well, Everett will be a hard act to follow. He is the best orator in the country. Will I have time to eat before I return to the train station?"

He shared his table with another reporter, and a local man. "If you want to cover a really interesting story, you should write about the ghost of Jennie Wade," the local suggested.

"Isn't she the young woman who was shot by a Confederate soldier while baking bread for our soldiers?" Thaddeus asked.

"There is no such thing as ghosts," the other reporter scoffed. "It is probably some poor deserter hiding in the bushes."

"Where is this ghost presently residing?" Thaddeus asked.

"Near the Schaeffer's home on Baltimore Street," the local replied pleased that this important reporter from New York was interested. Thaddeus had an idea.

There was a sizable crowd outside of the home of David Wills where the President, Edward Everett and other dignitaries were dining. President Lincoln briefly greeted the crowd.[4]

Thaddeus returned to the hotel to write an article and to plan his nocturnal investigation.

After midnight he gathered two biscuits wrapped in a napkin and quietly left the building. He did not look too conspicuous, for there were still people milling around. Fortunately, he found himself alone in the darkened silence in front of the Schaeffer's residence. Quietly, he walked through the backyard and the adjoining yards. He heard rustling in the bushes and placed the biscuits in front of some bushes before hiding behind a tree.

Within minutes, an emaciated soldier with a straggly beard and long matted hair appeared and picked up the biscuits. He bowed his head and gave thanks, "Father God, thank you for hearing my prayers and delivering this manna from heaven…"

That voice! It was the voice of the soldier who saved his life that night in July! He heard the bushes rustle as the soldier returned to his hiding place.

Thaddeus stepped out in front of the tree. "Your secret is safe with me. I will be back tomorrow night with much more food. Be safe. There will be thousands of people in town tomorrow. I will be back with food. I promise."

* * *

The next morning Thaddeus followed President Lincoln and Secretary of State William Seward as they visited part of the battlefield near the Seminary and returned to the Wills' home. Crowds began lining Baltimore Street in anticipation of the one-mile procession from the house to the cemetery.[5]

"Oh Pa, is this not exciting? There is the President!" Henry Gunther exclaimed.

"Yes, it is very exciting," his father agreed with a smile. There had not been much to smile about during the past four months, but Dedication Day would be long remembered.

The crowd clapped and cheered. He was followed by numerous dignitaries riding in carriages, military bands and soldiers dressed in their finest dress uniforms.

Thaddeus and over ten thousand people awaited the dignitaries in the cemetery. Finally, the honored guests arrived sitting on a special platform built for the occasion. Reverend T.H. Stockton opened with prayer followed by music by the marine band. The Honorable Ed Everett spoke eloquently for over two hours. As the crowd grew restless, many people began wandering around the fields. The Baltimore glee club followed with a hymn.[6]

Then President Lincoln stepped slowly and solemnly to the front of the platform.

Four score and seven years ago, our fathers brought forth on this continent, a new nation, conceived in Liberty, and dedicated to the proposition that all men are created equal.

Now we are engaged in a great civil war, testing whether that nation, or any nation so conceived and so dedicated, can long endure. We are met on a great battlefield of the war. We have come to dedicate a portion of that field, as a final resting place for those who gave their lives that this nation might live. It is altogether fitting and proper that we should do this.

But, in a larger sense, we cannot dedicate – we cannot consecrate – we cannot hallow- this ground. The brave men, living and dead, who struggled here, have consecrated it, far above our poor power to add or detract. The world will little note, nor long remember what we say here, but it can never forget what they did here. It is for us the living, rather, to be dedicated here to the unfinished work which they who fought here have thus far so nobly advanced. It is rather for us to be here dedicated to the great task remaining before us – that from these honored dead we take increased devotion to that cause for which they gave the last full measure of devotion – that we here highly resolve that these dead shall not have died in vain- that this nation, under God, shall have a new birth of freedom – and that government of the people, by the people, for the people, shall not perish from the earth."[7]

Thaddeus stood there speechless. Lincoln had said so much with so few words.

The ceremony ended with music and a closing prayer by Reverend H.L. Baugher. As the massive crowd dispersed and the dignitaries returned to the Wills' home for a late lunch and public reception,[8] Thaddeus remained reading the names of the Maine soldiers who gave their lives. He was relieved to see there were no Millers or Darian Flynn listed.

He later attended a speech by the Lt. Governor at the Gettysburg Presbyterian Church and then followed the President as he hurried to the train station.[9] He would spend the rest of the afternoon packing a straw basket with bread, cheese, apples and a jug of cider.

At midnight Thaddeus quietly left the Wagon Hotel with his basket and headed to the Schaeffer's backyard. As he approached the bushes he heard,

"The Lord is my shepherd;
I shall not want.
He makes me to lie down in green pastures;
He leads me beside the still waters.
He restores my soul;
He leads me in the paths of righteousness
For his name's sake"

Thaddeus quietly entered the bushes where he found the soldier kneeling with his eyes tightly shut. He put the basket down on the ground and knelt beside him.

"Yea, though I walk through the valley of the shadow of death,
I will fear no evil;
For You are with me;
Your rod and Your staff, they comfort me."

Now Thaddeus joined in and the two men recited,

"You prepare a table before me in the presence of my enemies;
You anoint my head with oil.
My cup runs over.
Surely goodness and mercy shall follow me
All the days of my life;
And I will dwell in the house of the Lord Forever." [10]

"I told you I would come back with more food," Thaddeus pointed to the basket. With dirty hands, the soldier hungrily broke the bread and offered a piece to Thaddeus. "I remember you. You are the private from Maine who saved my life back in July. What are you doing here?"

"Guard duty," he replied with his mouth full of food and took a sip of cider.

"What are you guarding?"

"The family," he pointed to the house. There are women and children and a baby. I have to stay here in case the Rebels return."

"Why don't you come back with me and sleep in a real bed and eat some hot food?"

"Can't leave my post. That would make me a deserter. They shoot deserters. I can't go back. I can't leave them unguarded. I can't. I can't." He began muttering and rocking back and forth. "I need it quiet…. quiet…quiet… Yes, it is quiet here."

"Private, if I find a soldier to relieve you of your post, would you come with me?"

"Never! They will send me back. I need it quiet…quiet…yes quiet…

Our Father Who art in heaven…"

"Suppose I take you back home to Maine. Maine is quiet. I know. I grew up in Fryeburg and …"

"Liar! Liar!" he shrieked. The wretched creature rocked back and forth.

"My name is Thaddeus Pierce, a grandson of Senator Benjamin Miller. I lived in my grandfather's big white house on the Main Street a few doors down from the Oxford Hotel. I sat in the Miller family pew in the front and center of the old Congregational Church. They built a new one since then. I sat with my grandparents, my parents, Joshua and Abigail Pierce, my Uncle Jacob, my cousins, Eli and…" He stopped and stared into the expressionless, gray eyes of the soldier. His heart began to pound. Even with the matted hair and tangled beard, the family resemblance was astonishing.

"You look exactly like your father. David Miller, I am here to take you home."

XVI

A Tale of Two Homecomings

Rachel glanced through the store window at the stagecoach stopped in front of the Oxford Hotel. She paid no attention to the two men who stepped out. The younger man pulled his jacket collar up, thrust both hands into his pockets and briskly walked away. The older man studied the old hotel as he waited for the driver to unload the luggage.

The five-story, pale yellow building with white columns looked the same. However, they had recently added a large two-story ell which contained additional guest rooms and stables. He grabbed his luggage and slowly walked down Main Street toward his grandparents' home.

Thaddeus stopped in front of the large white house at the corner. How many years had it been since his last visit? Could his grandparents still be alive? If so, they would be well into their nineties. He carried his luggage to the backyard and left them at the bottom of the back steps. He briskly knocked before entering the kitchen shouting, "Mama, am I late for supper?"

He was greeted by a frightened child wailing and an angry woman hitting him with a broom. "Get out! Get out of my house. How dare you enter my home uninvited and scaring my children! Out with you!"

"Madam, I assure you there must be some mistake. This is the home where I was raised. My parents own this house. My father's law office is here," Thaddeus explained as he jumped back narrowly missing a rap from the broom.

The woman stopped and glared at him. "Who are you?" she demanded.

"My name is Thaddeus Pierce, the grandson of Senator Miller and son of Joshua Pierce. And whom may you be?"

"I am Lydia Miller, the mistress of this home."

"Where are my parents? Have they moved?"

"They are both dead, killed in an accident. Now out!" she picked up the broom.

Thaddeus slammed the door behind him and ran down the steps. Picking up his luggage he headed to the Oxford Hotel.

* * *

It was Isaac who first saw David as he slowly walked toward the farm. "I do not believe my eyes! Eli! Eli! It's David."

"That old man is not my son," Eli squinted at the approaching figure.

Ignoring his brother, Isaac grabbed his cane and walked as fast as he could up the road. "David! David!" he waved his cane wildly.

David waved back.

"I cannot believe it!" Eli ran past Isaac yelling, "David! You have come home!" He embraced his son "Thank God! Thank God! You are home."

"Hello, Pa," he responded weakly.

"Your mother and I have been worried sick. Why did you not write?"

"I am sorry, Pa. I am very tired," he looked down on the ground.

"Welcome home, David," Isaac greeted.

David quickly looked up. "Isaac? You made it home?"

Isaac lifted his pants' leg revealing his wooden leg. "Most of me made it home," he joked.

"Is Monroe home?" he asked hopefully.

Isaac quickly glanced at Eli. "No. Are you hungry?"

David shook his head. "I am tired. I have a headache."

"Can you make it to the farm? You can rest there," Isaac suggested.

"Nonsense! He is coming home with me. His mother has been sick with worry!"

"Eli, run home and tell Julia the good news. David, let me help you to the farm. I know the journey can be exhausting."

Eli opened his mouth to protest before Isaac cajoled, "Eli, go tell Julia the good news!"

Jacob and Kate were standing on the front porch weeping openly. "David, you are home safe!" Jacob embraced his grandson.

"Look at you. You are all skin and bones! You come right in and let me feed you!" Kate put her arm through his and led him into the house. "This calls for Aunt Grace's best china in the dining room," she declared as she began pulling out dishes from the hutch. "It is only venison stew, biscuits and pumpkin pie," she apologized as she left for the kitchen.

"How did you make it home?" Isaac asked quietly.

"A man found me and took me home," David stared out the window.

"Found you where? You were missing for a long time." Isaac lowered his voice to a whisper, "David, did you desert?"

The door flew open and Julia came running in. "Davy! Davy!" and threw her arms around his neck.

David stiffened. "Mama, don't cry. Please don't cry."

* * *

Mr. Weston entered the general store and announced to Rachel, "There is a man at the Oxford Hotel drowning his sorrows claiming to be Thaddeus Pierce."

"Heavens! After all these years!" Rachel took off her apron, threw on her cloak and hat and ran across the street.

There were four men drinking at the bar. "Thaddeus?"

The well-dressed man with a neatly trimmed beard and mustache turned around, "Well, if it isn't my cousin the capitalist."

"We all thought you were dead!"

"I am sorry to disappoint you."

"We wrote you so many letters. When we wrote you that your parents were killed, and you never wrote back or visited we just assumed…" She covered her mouth with her hand. "I am so sorry. Did you hear of your parents' accident?"

"The young Mrs. Miller kindly informed me as she threw me out of my house."

"Grandpa offered you that house and law practice and you turned it down," she coldly reminded him. "It is Isaac's house now. Why did you come back today?"

"Do not worry. I have no intensions of staying. I brought Eli's boy home from Gettysburg. I plan to leave tomorrow."

"David is home!" Rachel left as abruptly as she had entered.

* * *

An hour later Daniel entered the bar and found Thaddeus sitting on the same stool. "Rachel told me I would find you here. Thad, I am so sorry about your parents. When Grandpa, Nana and Aunt Grace passed away, it was a great loss, but it was expected. It was such a shock when we heard about the accident three days after it happened. They went to Portland on business. When they did not return on the given day, we just assumed they were delayed. My father took it very hard. They were both very much admired and respected in Oxford County. The family is still grieving. I am truly sorry you had to learn about your loss under such unpleasant circumstances."

"Why are you not at the family reunion?" Thaddeus asked bitterly.

"I am, right here. We feared that both you and David were dead and now I discover that both of you are alive! We never forgot you. I wrote you plenty of letters. Where have you been all these years?"

"Let's see. Back in '54 I was at the Charge of the Light Brigade where I was reporting on the Crimean War. In '57 I was in India reporting on the mutiny of Indian troops against the British East Indian Company.[1]

I came back to America in '60 to cover the conventions and election and have been here ever since reporting on the war."

"Why did you not come to Fryeburg?"

"There are no battles in Fryeburg," he shrugged. "At least not the kind that involve bullets."

"Where did you find David?"

"At Gettysburg last week."

"But the battle was back in July. I arrived there nine days later."

Thaddeus turned to his cousin, "You were at Gettysburg? I thought you never left Fryeburg."

"I received a letter from Darian saying if we did not go to Gettysburg with medicine and supplies, Isaac would probably die. I spent weeks there looking for him."

"Did he? Did he die?"

"Thanks be to God, he did not. He had a leg amputated but he came home to his wife and daughters."

"And Darian?"

"Darian is a sharpshooter. He saved Isaac's life when he rescued him from a wheat field and brought him to a farmhouse where he received help." The pride was quite evident in his voice.

"He survived Gettysburg?"

"I hope so. We have not received any word since that letter. Any word about your sons?"

"I found them in eastern Europe. Their grandfather is a rabbi and he was not pleased to see me. He blamed me for the death of his daughter and forbade me to have any contact with them. My sons believe that their father was an Orthodox Jew who died a few months after he married their mother. I did meet them, but they do not speak English and my Yiddish is limited. I thought they looked like Eli's son. They definitely look like the Millers."

"I am sorry, Thad."

"I gave the rabbi all the money that I had and your name and address. I told them if they ever needed to escape to America to find you."

"Escape?"

"It is not safe to be a Jew in eastern Europe these days."

"Has it ever been safe to be a Jew?" Daniel questioned. "I am glad that you gave them my name."

"I knew I could depend on you."

"Were you in Gettysburg to write about the new cemetery? Did you see the President?"

"Indeed."

"How did you find David? Why was he still in Gettysburg?"

Thaddeus shrugged. "You will have to ask him that yourself."

"Come join me at the farm. We will celebrate the safe arrival of both of you."

He shook his head.

"Please come. The family will be so disappointed."

"It would not be the first time I disappointed them. It will be better for David if I stay away. It was good seeing you." He stood up, paid his tab and left.

* * *

When Daniel arrived at the farmhouse, he found the entire family crowded into the dining room. David sat quietly beside his mother unaware of the animated conversation around him. Daniel grabbed a bowl of stew and took a seat beside Eli.

"It was Thaddeus who found David and brought him home. You should go to the Oxford Hotel and talk to him," Daniel suggested.

"I will stop later. David, come join me tomorrow. I am going hunting. It will be just the two of us - just like the old days before the war," Eli invited.

Isaac intervened, "I think he might need a few days to rest. David, you look tired. Let me take you home. I still have my pocket New Testament. I will make you chamomile tea and read to you until you fall asleep. Would you like that?"

Eli gave Isaac a quizzical look. Julia put her hand on her son's arm, "David, are you sick?"

Mr. and Mrs. Quint knocked on the front door, entered the front hall and quickly arrived in the dining room. "We just heard that David is home!"

David stood up. "Hello Mr. and Mrs. Quint. You must be so proud of Monroe being awarded the Kearney Medal.[2] Have you heard from him recently?"

"David," Isaac tugged on his sleeve.

"Monroe is dead! He died in Gettysburg. Were you not there by his side? Where were you?" Mrs. Quint accused.

David began to tremble and sat down. He tightly closed his eyes and wiped the imaginary gore from his face with the back of his hand. "Monroe is dead?"

Isaac intervened, "Mrs. Quint, unless you were there, you cannot possibly understand. It is loud with cannon and gun fire. You cannot hear anyone talk or even yell. The battlefield is hazy with smoke, you cannot see clearly. Everyone looks alike in their blue uniforms. I am sure Monroe did not know that I was shot on July 2 even though we fought in the same regiment. People get separated during the chaos of battle. We do not eat or sleep for days. I am sure that David did not realize that Monroe was killed on the third."

"He died on the third?" he asked in a whisper. "Then it was not Monroe who was blown up and his torso landed on me," he muttered.

Mrs. Quint gasped in horror and ran out of the house.

"I am sorry, son," Mr. Quint looked at David with compassion. "I am sorry for all that you – both of you - have endured. I best be leaving."

The room fell silent. David tightly shut his eyes and trembled.

Isaac grabbed his cane and stood up. "Ma, can you make some chamomile tea, and can David lie down in Aunt Grace's bedroom?"

"I am tired," David whispered. "I am so tired."

"Get some rest before we take you home. I knew you were still alive. I never gave up hope," Julia shot a dirty look at her husband. "I knew you would come home." She slipped her arm through his and led him to the first-floor bedroom.

"Eli, you need to understand. Soldiers often go for days without eating or sleeping. It could take him weeks or months to get his strength back. He appears to be disoriented. He is very sensitive. He needs peace and quiet."

"What do you mean sensitive?"

"He found the loud canon blasts and the chaos of battle to be overwhelming. His nerves were frayed."

"Are you calling my son a coward?"

"No, he was very brave. He faced everyday square on. I am saying he needs rest."

"The important thing is he is home with us safe and sound," Jacob pronounced. "It took Isaac weeks to adjust and look how well he is doing. David will be fine in good time."

"Pa, I am going back to the Oxford Hotel to see Thaddeus. Do you care to join me?" Daniel invited.

"That sounds like a good idea."

* * *

They knocked on the door of his room. "It is open," Thaddeus called.

"Hello, Thad. Thank you for bringing my grandson home to me."

"Uncle Jacob!" He stood up and shook his hand. "Please have a seat," he offered him his chair while he sat on the bed.

"There are plenty of bedrooms back at the farm. You need not stay here. Please stay a few days. I had feared that I lost a son, a grandson and my sister's only child. And now all three of you are back home where you belong. I wrote you several letters, but you never wrote back. Just because your parents are gone, you are still a part of this family. You are always welcome here."

"Uncle Jacob, you and Danny are most kind and I appreciate it. I really do, but there is a war to report on and I must get back to work."

"Are you not tired of wars?" Jacob asked.

"Yes!" He hesitated before asking, "May I ask you two a personal question? Do you still believe in God? Danny, you have been to

Gettysburg. You have witnessed the carnage, the brutality, the savagery. How can a good God allow that?"

"He gave man a free will. Since Cain killed Abel, there has been bloodshed. Man's history is simply a history of man's wars. The question is not how a good God can allow war. The question is how a good God can still love such depraved men that he sent His Son to die on the cross for them. That is what I cannot understand.

Yes, I witnessed the horrible aftermath of battle. But I also witnessed, generosity, courage and compassion displayed to both Union and Confederate soldiers alike. Each of us has a choice to accept or reject His love."

"You missed your calling, cousin. You should have been a preacher."

"You asked. I answered."

"Uncle Jacob, how were my parents after I left?"

"To be honest, your mother was heart-broken. She talked about you all the time."

"And my father?"

"He too was heart-broken but he never mentioned your name. Each grieved in their own way."

Thaddeus stood up. "Thank you for visiting me, Uncle Jacob. I appreciate it. I promise I will write. But I need to leave first thing in the morning to catch the early coach to Portland and a train back to Washington."

"Thank you for bringing David home to us."

"Take care of him, Danny. He is damaged you know."

"I know. The important thing is that he is home."

* * *

An hour later there was another rap on the door. "It is open," Thaddeus called as Isaac entered. "I never realized that I was so popular."

"We are family. You cannot escape it. I looked up to you when I was growing up. You became your own person and not what your father expected you to be," Isaac confessed.

Thaddeus shrugged. "What is it with grandpa's cane?" he abruptly changed the subject.

"Lost my leg at Gettysburg. I was there with David. Where did you find him?"

"You should ask him that question."

"How did you find him?"

"He was hiding in the woods mumbling incoherently. I recognized his voice as the soldier who saved my life back in July. I brought food to him in the middle of the night. We talked awhile about Fryeburg and it was then I saw the Miller's curly brown hair and gray eyes. The boy looks just like Eli did at that age."

"How did you get him home?"

"I convinced him to come back to my hotel room. I gave him a bath, a haircut, a shave and burned his vermin ridden clothes. I hoped he would not run out of the hotel naked while I bought him some clothes. He slept the whole day. It was just a matter of buying train tickets."

"Did you tell anyone?"

"Did you mean did I tell anyone that a Miller is a deserter?"

"He is not a deserter. He is injured just as surely as I was. Tell no one. I will tell the family that you were writing a story about the closing of Camp Letterman and the transfer of the last of the patients. You heard of the story of the unidentified Union soldier who did not know who or where he was. Apparently, he was attacked by the retreating Confederates and left for dead. You were interviewing him for your newspaper article and when you realized he was from Fryeburg and recognized the family resemblance."

"Oh my, a Miller is going to tell a lie. Is that not breaking the Ten Commandments."

"I am the fourth generation of Millers circumventing the truth for the greater good. I am proud of that heritage."

"I am as well."

"Where are you going next?"

"Wherever the newspaper sends me. I telegraphed them that I had to return to Fryeburg for family business. They will send me to the next battle," he shrugged.

Isaac stood up to leave. "I will never forget what you did for David."

"Did what?" he feigned confusion and laughed. "Isaac, did you really admire me when you were a child?"

"Still do."

* * *

For the first time in his life Isaac sat in his grandfather's chair at his large mahogany desk. He took a sheet of parchment from the top drawer and a fountain pen. He stared at his discharge papers from Camp Letterman and studied the signature of Dr. Henry Janes. With great care and patience, he forged the discharge papers of Private David Frye Miller. He hoped his grandfather would approve.

XVII

The Adjustments

Eli woke with a start and looked at the sunlight streaming through the curtain. He had overslept. "Why did Julia not wake me? She knew I was planning to go hunting," he thought crossly. "That is so unlike her." A wave of fear swept over him as he realized something must be wrong. He quickly dressed and ran down the stairs where he found Julia wrapped in a wool shawl staring out the window.

She put her finger to her lips as she silently stepped back from the window. "He has been out there all night. He has your rifle and says he will shoot anyone who comes near," she whispered.

Eli headed to the door, "I will put an end to this nonsense right now."

Julia grabbed his arm. "That is not our son out there. There is something wrong – terribly wrong with him."

The approaching hoof beats interrupted their conversation. Through the kitchen window they could see David hold up his rifle. "No closer or I will shoot!" he yelled.

Isaac stopped his horse and waved a paper in his hand. "David, it is Isaac. Everything will be fine now. I have your discharge papers."

He put down the rifle. "What are you talking about?" he asked in bewilderment.

Isaac slid off the horse and slowly walked to his nephew, holding up the forged document. "Is there somewhere we can talk away from them?" he nodded toward the kitchen window. "How about the bridge? You can bring the rifle, but you will not need it," he assured as he handed him the paper.

"I do not understand," David shook his head.

"You are safe now. No one will make you go back. The army discharged you."

"How is this possible?"

"You are not a deserter any more than I am. I lost my leg and I can no longer fight. You lost your…"

"My courage? My mind? Are you saying that I am crazy?"

"This paper says you lost your memory because of injuries to your head. I say your soul has been wounded and needs to be healed. We have seen this in other soldiers. Soldiers' heart. Melancholy. I needed a wooden leg. You need peace, quiet and rest. That is all that I am saying. Our story is someone found you unconscious on Baltimore Street and brought you to a neighbor's house. You did not remember what happened to you or your name and they brought you to Camp Letterman, hoping someone would recognize you."

"A man recognized me in the woods."

"That is our cousin Thaddeus Pierce. His story, if anyone should ask, is he found you at Camp Letterman and recognized you as a Miller from Fryeburg."

"But I was never there. How did he get my discharge papers?"

"He did not. I copied mine and forged it."

"You could be shot if someone found out!" David protested

"We both would be shot," he corrected.

"Why would you risk your life for me now, when you are home safe with your family?"

"Because you need to be home safe with your family too. I am cold standing out here. Shall we go inside and have some coffee? Let me do all the talking and everything will be fine. Give me the rifle."

Julia flung open the kitchen door. "What is wrong?"

"I am sorry if I frightened you."

"We both could use a cup of coffee," Isaac tried to sound nonchalant. "Last night Thaddeus gave me these papers to give to

David. He says he is sorry that he missed you, but he had to take the first coach at sunrise to head back to Washington."

Julia was busy throwing firewood into the cookstove as the men sat down at the table. "I was telling David, that I too have problems sleeping at night. I think it was all the nights on patrol. The least little sound, the wind through the branches, a dog barking and you wake up thinking there is an army of rebels coming for you!

Since his injury, he sometimes forgets where he is. I saw that very often at Camp Letterman."

"What injury?" Julia asked as she ground the coffee.

Isaac repeated the story. "Thad said, if David did not look just like you, Eli – or the way he remembered you – he might still be in the hospital. His memory seems be coming back. Doctors say in cases like this, rest and quiet are the best medicine."

"I am sorry, Pa. I thought I was guarding the house. I was expecting the enemy to come find me. I need to go to bed." He rose from the table and slowly ascended the stairs.

Julia handed Isaac his coffee. "Thank you, Julia. It will take time. Be patient. I have been home for months and I still struggle. I cannot bear to feed the hogs. Starving pigs roamed wild eating amputated limbs or digging up bodies from shallow graves."

Julia gasped and covered her mouth. "Isaac, this is not talk for a lady to hear," Eli chastised.

"No. I need to hear this. I need to understand," she argued.

"No one can understand what war is like unless you have been there yourself. But you can be patient. Eli, David has killed enemies and watched friends die. I know you meant well, but I do not think he will enjoy hunting for quite some time. You need to be patient and do not ask questions. He will come around in his own way in his own time."

* * *

David looked around at his family gathered around his grandmother's dining room table. "I do not understand. Why are we having Sunday dinner on Thursday afternoon?"

"President Lincoln declared today as a day of Thanksgiving for the whole country," Eli repeated patiently. Julia had explained that to him twice earlier this morning.

"I think it is wonderful that the family joined together for this meal. We have not had the opportunity to visit with you," Daniel said cheerfully. "I am most grateful that the Lord saw fit to spare the lives of my brother and nephew. It gives me hope that Darian will be coming home one day."

"I am thankful for our injuries," Isaac looked at David. "Because of our injuries we were able to return home instead of fight."

"For one day, there will be no talk of war," Kate admonished from the kitchen. Julia brought in a platter of venison, Lydia carried a tureen of butternut squash soup and Emily placed a bowl of boiled potatoes on the table. Summer had a basket of biscuits while Mahayla brought in the butter and Emily a large bowl of applesauce.

The family bowed their heads as Jacob prayed. "Lord, everything we have comes from you. We thank you for our homes, our food, our families. I pray for your mercy and comfort on the Quint family and all the families both North and South who are mourning the loss of their loved ones. I pray that you will be with Darian and all the other soldiers who are away from their families. May this terrible war soon be over. May you restore this nation. Amen."

Platters and bowls were passed in an orderly fashion.

"Me and Summer made the applesauce," Mahayla proudly announced.

"Summer and I made the applesauce," Lydia corrected.

"You did not make the applesauce. Me and Summer spent the afternoon at Nana's," she argued.

"Mama was correcting your grammar. You must speak correctly when you go to school," Summer informed her younger sister.

Mahayla merely rolled her eyes in response.

"You know, I never ate a potato until Darian came to the family," Jacob reminisced. "When he returns home from the war, we will have another Thanksgiving dinner just for him."

"I like butternut squash better," Mahayla interrupted.

"Ladies do not speak with their mouths full and children do not interrupt adults," Lydia quietly corrected her daughter.

"I am thankful for Danny and Emily and all their help," Lydia turned to her sister-in-law and best friend.

"I am thankful for my new business venture. I do not think I was meant to be a farmer," Isaac confessed.

Jacob saw Eli's angry scowl at his brother.

"Much to my father's disappointment, I was not meant to be a lawyer," Jacob chuckled. "Much to my grandfather's disappointment, my father was not meant to be a farmer."

"I was not meant to be soldier," David said quietly as he tightly closed his eyes and shook his head.

"Cousin Davy, would you like some more applesauce? You cannot be sad and eat applesauce at the same time," Mahayla passed the bowl.

David opened his eyes and smiled. "Only one thing could make me happier than applesauce. That is to give my cousins a ride on the toboggan."

Mahayla's squeal of delight filled the room. "Girls, finish your meal, take your dishes to the kitchen and then I will help you bundle up," Lydia offered. She mouthed the words "thank you" to David who smiled and winked back.

"When I am done eating, I will get the toboggan, snowshoes and bear skin rug from the barn," David added.

"Cousin Davy, I am glad you did not lose your leg in the war," Mahayla patted his hand. No one else in this family is any fun."

It took at least fifteen minutes to get the girls dressed and situated before they left waving and giggling.

"I roasted some coffee beans last night. Would anyone care for coffee and apple pie?" Kate offered.

"Mother Miller, please sit and enjoy your family. You have been busy for the past two days. I will grind the beans and make the coffee," Lydia offered. "Coffee is all Isaac will drink."

"Other than the packages of tea Mama sent us, coffee was all we had to drink in the army. It was not very good, but it was all we had," he explained.

"It appears that David is doing better," Jacob tried to sound encouraging.

"He has his good and bad moments," Julia admitted.

"He seems to enjoy spending time with the girls," Emily observed.

"Give him time. I think his good moments will begin to outnumber his bad ones," Isaac predicted.

"I hope you are right."

* * *

It was the first week of December when Rachel saw the letter. "Peter! A letter from Darian. He is in Virginia."

"What are you waiting for? Go!" Peter handed his wife her cloak and hat, hitched the horse to the sleigh and sent Rachel and the letter east toward the lumber mill.

Upon arrival, she knocked on the kitchen door and rushed in. "Emily! Danny!" she called excitedly waving the letter.

"Gracious. The sun is not yet up!" Emily spied the envelope. "A letter? A letter from Darian?"

"The answer to our prayers!" Daniel took the letter.

Danny,

Did you get my letter? Did you find Isaac? Is he alive?

I was captured by retreating soldiers in Gettysburg and have been in Libby Prison in Richmond for the past five months. It is a very large brick building that once served as a warehouse.[1] Tell Emily not to worry. Prison is no worse than my army camp and no one is shooting at us. They are negotiating a prisoner exchange and I hope to be out soon. A nice minister's wife brought paper and pens, so we could write home for Christmas. Please write soon for I am most anxious to hear from the family.

Darian

"What is wrong?" Rachel asked.

"Darian has been in a prison in Richmond since July," Emily quietly replied.

"I am truly sorry for that, but at least we know he is not dead. He is not fighting and not in danger," Rachel tried to encourage her sister-in-law.

"How true!" Daniel agreed. "Look at all we can be thankful for. I am declaring this to be a holiday – a letter writing holiday," he declared. "Now let us tell the rest of the family."

Dear Darian,

You are the best friend a man could have. You saved my life and Danny did receive your letter. It took weeks, but he found me and when I was ready, he took me home.

You will not recognize the girls; they have grown so much. Summer is already in school. You would be quite impressed with my new wooden leg. I have left farming to become a traveling apothecary. I am building a peddler's wagon and Lydia, Mahayla, my mother and I are preparing remedies to be sold this spring.

David made it back home. Unfortunately, Monroe was killed on the last day of the battle. I am making this letter short, so it will go into the afternoon post.

Your devoted friend,
Isaac

Dear Darian,

I can never repay you for saving my husband's life. You are the bravest man I know.

Gratefully,
Lydia

Dear Darian,

After I received your letter in July, I left that very afternoon for Gettysburg. I could have never imagined the magnitude of the destruction, the violence, the suffering, if I had not seen it for myself! The people of Gettysburg are the most generous and courageous people I have ever met. I also had the privilege of working with selfless and faithful volunteers from all over the North.

After witnessing that carnage, I do not understand how all of you soldiers can bear such horrors. Thaddeus found David at a military hospital during a visit to Gettysburg while he was writing about the dedication of a new national cemetery. I fear his spirit has been crushed and his mine tortured by the ravishes of war.

Emily and I pray for you every day. We hope to hear about your release in the prison exchange.

I am so proud of your desire to defend our country. Running the mill without your help is but a small sacrifice compared to the sacrifices made by you, Isaac, David and all our soldiers.

I am enclosing some paper and pen with hopes we will hear from you soon.

Gratefully,
Danny

By late afternoon no fewer than eight letters and three packages were mailed.

* * *

The Miller clan, minus Rachel and her family, sat in the front and center pew at the Congregational Church singing the last verse of "It Came Upon a Midnight Clear" at the Christmas Eve service.

"You are all welcome to come back to the farm for hot mulled cider and spice cake," Kate invited.

Mahayla knew that meant Nana and Grandpa had presents for them. As excited as she was, she refrained from squealing because they were still in church. She would have to wait until the ride home.

"David, having you sit next to me in church is the best Christmas gift a grandfather could wish for. All we need is for Darian to come home," Jacob patted him on the back.

Last week was the first time David felt well enough to attend church. However, it was only the promise that Isaac would sit next to him near the back door that gave him the courage to go. Then he quickly slipped out the door before the completion of the last hymn. Tonight, was different. He sat next to his grandfather in the front of the church. He felt uncomfortable for he imagined that everyone was staring at him. But he did it. Maybe Isaac was right. All he needed was quiet, rest and time. After the service he gripped his grandfather's arm as they walked down the crowded center aisle.

As the sleighs pulled up to the front of the farm Kate exclaimed, "Mercy, Jacob! The parlor is on fire!" as she pointed to the window. Flickering flames could be seen in the corner of the room.

Eli, David and Daniel jumped off the sleighs and ran into the house followed by the rest of the family.

"Merry Christmas!" Rachel, Peter and the boys greeted.

Jacob sank onto the old settee. "We thought the house was on fire."

"What is this?" Kate demanded.

"Mama, it is a Christmas tree," Rachel explained. "The boys and I strung popcorn and cranberries. We made bows from remnants of white and red fabrics. When we heard the church bells ringing, I began to light the candles. It is perfectly safe. See how the candle holders are held on by a metal clasp. We have sold hundreds of these small white candles and candle holders."

"Why is a tree inside my house? Trees belong outside," Jacob shook his head.

"Papa, Queen Victoria puts up and decorates a tree every year. It is a German tradition that Prince Albert brought with him to England from Germany."[1]

"Worshipping trees is a pagan tradition," Daniel argued.

"It was Martin Luther who lit candles on an evergreen tree to demonstrate that Jesus was the Light of the World,"[2] Rachel countered.

"We are neither Lutherans nor Germans. Your grandmother was a Quaker. Your grandfather was quite proud of his Pilgrim roots," Jacob protested.

Kate saw the disappointment on her grandsons' faces. "I think it is lovely. Perhaps this generation will begin some new Miller family traditions."

"I think it is peaceful. I could look at this tree for hours," David stated as he sat on the floor by the tree.

"I think it is beautiful! It is like the tree is wearing stars!" Mahayla sat beside David mesmerized by the candlelight.

"Well then, that settles it. Merry Christmas!" Jacob laughed.

* * *

David rocked back and forth in his mother's rocking chair gazing out the parlor window not seeing the gray skies and mounds of snow. He held a half-filled cup of chamomile tea in one hand and a battered New Testament in the other. Quiet…Quiet… He needed quiet as he whispered the Lord's Prayer.

The silence was shattered when the kitchen door flew open and slammed shut.

"Goodness, Mahayla, where are your hat and mittens? It must be zero degrees outside!" Julia scolded as she threw more wood into the cookstove.

"I am running away from home and staying here!" she declared with a stomp of her foot.

"Why? What happened?"

"They said that I am impossible!"

"Who said that?"

"Everybody. Even Nana." Tears streamed down her frozen, rosy cheeks.

The sound of sleigh bells grew louder as Isaac neared the house. A moment later he stood in the warm kitchen.

"I do hope you did not travel all this way to apologize for I shall not accept your apology!" Mahayla pouted.

A chuckle could be heard from the front parlor.

"No, I did not come to apologize. I came to take you back to the farm," her father firmly stated.

"Why do I have to sew those stupid bags? I do not like sewing."

No one heard David rise from his seat and stand in the kitchen doorway. "I know how to sew. I can teach you," he offered.

"You will?"

"I like sewing. It is quiet."

"I fear sewing with Mahayla will be anything but quiet," Isaac warned.

"Nana can make us tea and we can sit by the wood stove and be warm and sew," she ignored her father's comment.

"We need dozens of muslin bags to package our teas. I hope to have the wagon filled, organized and ready to leave right after mud season," Isaac explained.

David nodded, "I can help you. I can sew and build shelves for the wagon. I can help."

"I am most thankful because I certainly can use all the help I can get!"

* * *

The March sunshine was slowly melting the snow as David and Mahayla continued with their sewing. Unlike the rest of the family, he found his cousin's cheerful chattering to be a pleasant distraction from his dark thoughts.

"Papa says you are a very brave soldier and you won a medal."

"Your papa and my friend, Monroe, won medals too you know."

"He never told me that. Papa says you hurt your head in the war and that is why you get headaches and take rests and like quiet. The doctor cut Papa's leg off. I am glad the doctor did not cut off your head. I do not think a wooden head would work, do you?"

"I would have to agree with you."

"Papa says you were the smartest boy in Fryeburg Academy and someday you will become President. I want to vote for you, but Aunt Rachel says girls are not allowed to vote. I do not think that is fair, do you?"

"No, I do not."

Eli entered the house announcing, "The sap is running!"

Mahayla dropped her sewing. "Come on, Davy!"

"I am not sure," he stammered.

"Collecting sap is very quiet. Grandpa's old knees do not work, and Papa's wooden leg does not walk on snowshoes. Let's face it, Uncle Eli is no spring chicken, either. We need you, Davy. Please!"

"I guess I can help," he offered reluctantly.

"We need you, Davy. The family really, really needs you."

XVIII

Secrets

David shivered in the semi-darkness as he paced in front of his house. It was April; the snow was rapidly melting, and hungry bears were awakening from their hibernation. He stopped in his tracks as he heard the crackling of branches in the distance. He strained his eyes in the dawn's light to see a large black shape lumber out of the woods. A splash told him the bear had entered the Saco River. He could now clearly see the black creature against the snow shaking herself dry and bound toward the farm.

The livestock! He gripped the rifle as he ran across Weston's Bridge. In the distance he heard chickens frantically squawking and a wooden spoon pounding against an iron pot. "Scat! Scat! Get a move on!" he heard his grandfather's voice.

"No, Grandpa! Get back in the house. They are only chickens. Get back in the house!" he shouted as he ran through the fields toward the hen house.

"Jacob? What is going on?" he heard his grandmother call from the back porch.

"Nana get back in the house!" he screamed as he entered the yard. He suddenly stopped as the hungry bear, angered by the interruptions, stood on her hind legs and roared. His grandfather dropped the pot.

David sighted his rifle. "I'm too far away. Darian could take the shot but…" He did not have time to think. He pulled the trigger just as the bear lunged forward. His grandmother screamed, and his grandfather jumped to the side just as the beast crashed to the ground.

"You, old fool! You could have been killed!" Kate burst into tears.

David was shocked! He never heard his grandmother speak like that before. Jacob hobbled over to his wife as quickly as he could. "Please, Katie, do not cry. I am sorry. I will never do a reckless thing like that again. David, you saved my life! You saved your foolish old grandfather's life."

"Grandpa, please do not talk like that," he ran up onto the porch.

"David, you are trembling. Come inside and warm up," Kate had regained her composure.

"Thank you, Nana. Could you make me some chamomile tea? I will bury the dead chickens. It looks like that bear tore the door of the hen house right off the hinges. I need to repair the door."

"I will get some tools from the barn," Jacob offered.

David surveyed the damage. There were feathers, blood and entrails everywhere. Six dead chickens – parts of six dead chickens were strewn throughout the yard. A bloodied rooster who was missing a wing, his beak and an eye, ran in circles screeching.

"Shut up!" David yelled. "I said shut up! Shut up!" He put the barrel of the rifle to the bird's head and pulled the trigger. The screeching stopped as feathers flew through the air."

Isaac was eating breakfast when he heard the gunshots and screaming in the distance. "It sounds like it is coming from the farm!" He grabbed his cane and rifle and limped out the door.

"Be careful!" Lydia called out as her husband mounted his horse and galloped up the road. Isaac followed the sounds of sobbing to the hen house and found David sitting on the ground, holding his head in his hands.

"I killed him. I could not stand his screaming, so I killed him."

Jacob stood by helplessly holding some lumber and a hammer.

"Come in for tea, David. This has been a big shock for all of us. Please come in and warm up. You will catch a chill," Kate pleaded.

Eli came running down the road. "I heard gun shots and I was afraid that…" He stopped at the sight of the bear and whistled. He turned to his son still seated on the ground. "You killed it?"

"I had to. I had no choice," he whispered as he stared at the dead rooster.

"He saved my life! That bear was on her hindlegs ready to pounce. I was saying my prayers when I hear a crack and the bear falls right to the ground. The Good Lord knew I did not have the sense to stay inside so he brought home my grandson to protect me."

"I have never been so proud of you, son," Eli helped David to his feet. It did not matter that some people in the village whispered that David was a deserter or crazy or a coward. It did not matter that he refused to go hunting or refused to leave the house for days. It did not matter that he sometimes paced in front of the house muttering to himself at night. His son was a hero and saved his grandfather's life.

"Eli, what happened?" Julia panted as she ran into the yard. "I heard gunshots."

"Everything is fine, dear. Our son shot that bear and saved my father's life."

Julia threw her arms around her son's neck. "Thank God you are all right."

"Please come in out of the cold and have some tea," Kate shivered as she opened the back door.

The family sat around the kitchen table warming by the cookstove.

"I am tired," David shut his eyes and shook his head. "Thank you for the tea. I would like to go home and to bed."

"I say you deserve a nap after this morning," Jacob smiled in gratitude. "I could use one myself."

"I will walk you home," Isaac offered as he stood up.

"I need to pick up a few things at the general store," Eli also stood up.

David silently walked out the kitchen door with Isaac following.

* * *

Eli was pleased to see the store was crowded when he entered. "Peter, I just stopped by in case Rachel was worried about hearing the gunshots at the farm," Eli stated loudly.

"Rachel came out of the back room. "Gunshots? Did somebody say gunshots?"

Several people stepped closer to the counter. "David tracked a bear from the woods, over the river to the farm. She ripped the hen house door right off the hinges and just helped herself. My father came out banging a pan to scare it off."

"Always worked for me," Mr. Osgood approved. Several others nodded in agreement.

"It did not work this time. That bear stood up on her hind legs ready to attack. Just then David comes running up with my rifle. One shot. It never knew what hit it."

"Ain't that something," Mr. Charles exclaimed.

"After killing his fair share of Rebels, killing an unarmed bear is easy," Eli bragged.

* * *

"Wait. You know I cannot keep up!" Isaac called out.

David waited on the covered bridge staring at the rushing river.

"I am grateful to you. The thought of having Ma helplessly watch my father being mauled to death…" His voice trailed off. "I am sorry that you had to witness the damage. It must have brought back some terrible memories."

"I killed him, Isaac. He would not stop screaming, so I put the rifle to his head and put him out of his misery." He started sobbing. "I am going to burn in hell."

Isaac gingerly put his hand on his shoulder. "It was just a rooster."

"I am not talking about the rooster. I am talking about the Confederate soldier. His unit just left him. He was shot in the stomach and in agony. He would not stop screaming so I killed him."

Isaac nervously ran his fingers through his hair. "It is war. They kill us. We kill them."

"This was not on the battlefield. It was after the battle. He did not even have a gun. I told him that it would be over soon. I put the gun to his head and…" He tightly shut his eyes and shook his head. "I am going to burn in hell, Isaac."

What would Danny say in a case like this? "God forgives us if we repent. Remember the story of Saul of Tarsus? They were stoning Stephen and he stood there and approved. God forgave him, and Saul was called Paul and preached the gospel all over the Roman world. And remember the thief on the cross? He was guilty and was right next to Jesus. He said he was sorry, and Jesus said that he would go to Paradise.

The fact you feel guilty is a good sign. It would be worse if you did not care. I think more soldiers than we care to admit on both sides have done what you did. I think you just need to tell God that you are sorry."

"You won't tell anyone, will you? Promise me."

"I can keep a secret. I promise.

* * *

Isaac awoke to the sound of rapping on the kitchen door. He quickly put on his leg, walked into the kitchen and opened the door. "Eli, what on earth are you doing? It is the middle of the night!"

"David is missing. I have looked everywhere," he replied frantically.

"When was the last time you saw him?" he whispered.

"He went to bed right after supper. He said he was tired."

"When did you notice he was missing?"

"Two hours ago. I have looked everywhere. The horses are still here. He cannot go too far."

"He will not walk alone to the general store in daylight. I cannot imagine he would go far at night."

"I told you I have looked everywhere."

"Then we will look again." Isaac grabbed another lantern and the brothers quietly left.

"I will check the barn. You better wake up Pa. Maybe David is spending the night with them."

"I already checked the barn."

"Did you check the hayloft? He might be sleeping up there." Eli opened the barn door and Isaac held up his lantern. "Get out, Eli! Get out of here!" Isaac yelled. A shadowy figure hung from a rope high up in the rafters.

"No! Davy! Davy!!" Eli yelled as he climbed the ladder to the hay loft. He cut the rope with his knife and the body hit the floor with a sickening thud.

Isaac knelt by his nephew's body and gently removed the noose.

"Why? Why?" Eli sobbed. "How could you do this to us? How could you?" He turned to Isaac with a wild look in his eyes. "Julia must never know! No one must ever know!"

Isaac nodded in agreement. "The truth will not bring him back. It will only break his mother's heart, disgrace his memory and ruin the Millers' good name. It is too late for the truth. We will make it look like an accident. Break that old railing," Isaac pointed to the hay loft. "One good kick should do it. Then position it under his body so it will look like the railing broke and he fell backwards to his death." He took David's cold hand. "I am sorry, David. May you and Monroe rest in peace."

They repositioned the body and broken rail to make it look like an accident.

"Go back to bed. I will burn the rope in the cookstove. Then you will discover the body at daybreak," Isaac instructed.

"You have to keep this a secret!" Eli threatened.

"Don't worry, I am good at keeping secrets."

* * *

Relatives, friends and town's people crowded the front parlor of River View Farm. Eli sat silently by his son's closed, pine casket. He stared down at the floor seeing nothing. Isaac sat protectively beside his brother. Daniel sat on the other side of Isaac patting Jacob's arm. Respectful silence filled the parlor.

In contrast, the kitchen was brimming with activity. Kate supervised as her daughter and daughters-in-law piled food on platters and set them on the dining room table. "Julia, please do not tire yourself," Emily pleaded.

"It helps to keep busy. This is the last meal I will ever make for my son. I need to do this."

Upstairs a little girl sobbed, "Davy! Davy! I don't want you to be dead!"

* * *

The Congregational Church was a sea of black, filled with mourners. The extended Miller family had filled the front pews numerous times for family funerals. Today the Wiley family, Kate's siblings, cousins, nieces and nephews filled the pews on the right. The Fryes, Julia's parents, siblings, cousins, nieces and nephews filled the pews on the left. Emily's family, the Walker clan sat behind the Millers. Julia's daughters, Rebecca and Victoria, sat beside her with their husbands and children. Julia was greatly comforted by their presence. Eli did not listen to Pastor Sewall's sermon, encouraging words or prayers.

A parade of mourners slowly followed the wagon carrying David Miller's casket down Main Street and into the cemetery behind the stone schoolhouse. Someone had thoughtfully set a few benches for the elderly to sit upon. Jacob and Kate gratefully took a seat as Jacob studied the gravestones before him.

The simple slate stone in the center belonged to his grandparents, James and Sarah Miller, one of the early settlers of the town. Next to theirs was a small stone for Abigail Miller, twin sister of Benjamin Miller who died at the age of twelve in the year 1780. To the right stood the ornate, granite gravestone for his Uncle Micah and Aunt Grace. Grace Miller made certain that her husband would have a stone worthy of her husband. To the left of his grandparents stood a tall, imposing stone marking the resting place of Senator Benjamin James Miller, his father and his godly, modest mother Hannah. Next to his parents' grave stood a more modest stone for his sister Abigail and her husband, Joshua. There was a plot reserved for Kate and him. David was supposed to bury him. No grandfather should have to bury his grandson.

Mr. and Mrs. Frye stoically sat on the other bench. Many Fryes had fought in America's wars. Joseph Frye was awarded a land grant from King George for his service to the crown in the French and Indian War. This land became the town of Fryeburg. He and his sons served in the American Revolution. Today his descendants were fighting in the War between the States.

Mrs. Quint, still dressed in black, stood nearby silently weeping. "It was like losing a second son," she had confided to Julia the day before.

Julia linked arms with her daughters; her youngest granddaughter held tightly onto her skirt. "At least I had six months with my son before he died. I can take comfort in knowing where he is. The poor Quint family only knows that Monroe is buried somewhere in that big cemetery in Gettysburg. They will probably never see their son's grave," Julia thought. Her heart may have been broken, but her spirit was strong.

Four of David's Frye cousins slowly lowered the casket into the ground. Eli stood staring straight ahead. Isaac felt flush and his knees grow weak. Lydia helped him sit on the bench beside his mother. He covered his face with his hands. "God, please don't send him to hell. He could not help it. He did not mean to kill the Confederate soldier. He did not mean to kill himself. He was sick. Let me take his place. I knew better but I lied. I knew better. It is my fault he is dead. I should have not left him alone. Send me to hell instead," he pleaded silently.

Kate protectively put her arm around her grieving son. Eli glanced at them in disdain. "Mama's boy!" he seethed.

Unexpectedly Daniel walked to the grave site. "It seems like only yesterday my family was gathered here to bury my dear grandmother, Hannah Miller. During the sermon Reverend Hurd preached, 'I am the resurrection, and the life: he that believeth in me, though he were dead, yet shall live.' That evening, Davy – we called him Davy when he was still a child – asked me what did that mean? How do we know Nana was good enough to go to Heaven?

I explained that no one is good enough to go to Heaven. Romans says, 'for all have sinned and come short of the glory of God.' The reason we know that Nana is in heaven is that Jesus took her place. He paid for her sins on the cross. That is why we can be confident that she is heaven. Then Davy asked me how he could be sure that he would go to Heaven. I told him it was simple. He simply had to believe that he indeed was a sinner, that he could not enter the Kingdom of Heaven based on his good deeds. He needed to believe that Jesus was truly the Son of God, confess our sins and ask Jesus to take away his sins.

Not only the sins committed by a dear child, but all his future sins would be covered as well. That is why I can stand here both broken hearted over the loss of my dear nephew and rejoicing that I know that he is at peace for eternity. I wanted Eli, Julia and his sisters to be reassured."

Isaac sat up straight and watched Daniel return to his place by Emily. Today David Frye Miller found his Quiet.

XIX

Andersonville Prison Letters

Rachel held the envelope in her hand. "Daniel received a letter from St Stephens Episcopal Church in Virginia. Do you think Darian is dead? Is that why the church is writing to inform us of his death? Is that why we never heard back from him?" she fought back the tears.

"We need to deliver this to the lumber mill right away," Peter responded solemnly. "I will close the store."

Rachel put on her shawl and bonnet while Peter hitched the horse to the wagon. It was a beautiful May morning and Peter was thankful that mud season was finally over.

They rode silently. "First David's death, was Darian dead as well?" Rachel thought gloomily. Eli spoke to no one since the funeral. Her parents were deeply grieved over their grandson's death. Isaac tried to be strong for the rest of the family, but Darian's death would crush him.

Daniel greeted them in the side yard. "You must have a letter for me. It has been over five months since his last letter and Emily and I were growing anxious. I prayed that we would receive word from him soon," he accepted the letter from Peter. His smile soon turned to a frown.

"Please come in for some tea. Emily needs to read this."

The three of them found Emily in the kitchen baking bread. "This can only mean one thing. We must have a letter from Darian." She brushed the flour from her hands before taking the letter.

To Whom It May concern,

I feel it is my Christian duty to inform you that your loved one is no longer a resident of our fair city. The prisoner of war exchange never occurred. The Yankee prisoners have been shipped south to Georgia to a newly constructed facility. While our brave sons give their lives fighting a war against northern aggression, your sons enjoyed a holiday in the warmth of a Georgia winter.

I pray that this horrible war will soon come to an acceptable end and all our sons will soon come home.

"What does this mean?" Emily asked fearfully.

"It means the South is worried that Richmond will fall to the Union. If this should happen, hundreds of prisoners would once again be free to fight. The only prudent action on their part would be to ship these men as far south as possible," Rachel explained with a sigh of relief.

"But why did the prisoner exchange fall through?" Emily asked.

"The two parties could not come to an agreement as to what to do with the Negro soldiers," Rachel could not hide her anger. "The South refused to treat the black prisoners the same as whites."

"I will read through all of our old newspapers and look for articles about a new prison camp in Georgia," Peter offered. "Now we understand why we have not heard from him. I wonder if he ever received any of our letters."

"I think the family should continue our letter writing and mail them all at once when we learn of Darian's new location," Daniel tried to conceal his disappointment from Emily.

April 1864
Miller & Flynn Lumber Mill
Fryeburg, Maine

Dear Darian,

We only learned today that you have moved to Georgia. We hope you received all our letters before you left. If not, please know that I did receive your letter in July, and I left for Gettysburg that very day. I found Isaac alive in an army hospital and brought him home weeks later. I will let Isaac write about his life at home.

Peter is hoping to learn more about this prison camp and find an address to write you. In the meantime, we will continue to write and save our letters.

I have been reading in the Bible about some godly men who the Lord used in prison. Do you remember the story of Joseph, the son of Jacob? His jealous brothers sold him into slavery. In Egypt, he was falsely accused of an immoral act and thrown in prison. Yet, it was part of God's plan. When Pharaoh needed a dream to be interpreted, one of Joseph's former prison mates remembered Joseph. After Joseph interpreted the dream, the Pharaoh made him an official, saved the country from famine and eventually saved his entire extended family.

He did not give up in despair when he was in prison, for he remained faithful to the God of his family. He had no way of knowing at the time, that his prison stay was merely temporary, a small step towards God's grand design for Joseph's life.

Then there was Daniel. What a sad day that must have been for this Jewish teenage boy, when the Babylonians conquered and destroyed Jerusalem before taking Daniel and thousands of other Jews into captivity. He was thrown into a pagan world of foreign languages, unfamiliar customs, cultures, food and religion. Not only did he remain faithful to his God, he was appointed as one of King Nebuchadnezzar's wise men. He never returned to Jerusalem, but he made a godly impact on those around him.

Perhaps the best-known prisoner in the Bible is the Apostle Paul. While he was preaching the Gospel throughout the Roman empire, he was sent to a prison in Rome. He had planned to visit Spain, not sit in jail. Yet, he did not despair. It was there in a Roman prison that Paul wrote the books of Ephesians, Philippians, Colossians and Philemon.

Yet while he was in chains, he wrote in the fourth chapter of Philippians,

"Rejoice in the Lord always: again I say, Rejoice

Let your moderation be known unto all men. The Lord is at hand.

Let your moderation be known unto all men. The Lord is at hand.

Be careful for nothing; but in everything by prayer and supplication with thanksgiving let your requests be made known unto God.

And the peace of God, which passeth all understanding, shall keep your hearts and minds through Christ Jesus.

Finally, brethren, whatsoever things are true, whatsoever are honest, whatsoever things are just, whatsoever things are pure, whatsoever things are lovely, whatsoever things are of good report; if there be any virtue, and if there be any praise, think on these things."

You have not been abandoned or forsaken. The God of Joseph, Daniel and Paul is by your side.

Devotedly,
Danny

Two days later Peter arrived at the farm with several newspapers. "Last November, a small village in southern Georgia was chosen to build a Confederate prison for Union soldiers.

The most information that I can gather is there is a sixteen-acre plot surrounded by a stockade of hewed line logs built by slaves. It is near the railroad and has a supply of fresh water. The name of this place is Andersonville Prison."[1] Looking at a pile of newly written letters on the kitchen table he offered, "Would you like me to mail a few of these?"

Three weeks later a brief letter from Darian arrived.

Dear Family,

I was quite relieved to hear that Isaac made it home. That was weighing on my mind for months. I arrived here in late February or early March.[2] I am losing track of time.

My biggest complaint is I am hungry all the time. I will never complain about hardtack and camp food again! Every night I dream of Mrs. Miller's kitchen and all the meals we have enjoyed over the years. Then I remind myself that I survived the Great Hunger in Ireland and I will survive this as well.

Has anyone heard from David?

Please keep writing even If you do not hear back from me right away. Your words are a lifeline.

Yours,
Darian

While the family rejoiced over this letter, it did not lessen the pain of losing David. Jacob sat down and struggled to find the words to write.

May 1864
River View Farm
Fryeburg, Maine

Dear Darian,

I wept with joy when we received your letter. It is with great sadness that I write our David died in an accident. Thaddeus surprised us all back in November when he came to visit and brought David home with him. The poor lad suffered an injury to the head and needed much quiet and rest. Nevertheless, he was back home with the family and we celebrated Thanksgiving and Christmas together. He was even able to help Isaac and Lydia set up their new business and join the family tapping trees. One morning he saved my life by killing a bear in the backyard that was ready to attack! Eli was so proud. The next morning Isaac and Eli found David on the floor of the barn. It appears that he fell out of the hayloft and broke his neck.

There are days I struggle to understand how this happened. There are other days I am simply thankful for the time we had with him, that he died here and not some faraway battlefield and he is buried in the family plot.

Now I learned that you are alive. Be strong and come home to us for the family needs you. I pray this horrendous war will end soon and we will be reunited.

Grandfather Miller

May 1864
The Benjamin Miller House
Fryeburg, Maine

Dear Darian,

Thank God you are alive. I need your advice. I lied. My grandmother would never approve but, yet I see no other solution. David was a deserter. It really was not his fault. He had a terrible case of soldier's heart and melancholy. I forged his discharge papers to make it look like he was suffering from confusion and memory loss from a head injury. No one questioned it. Back in April he was inconsolable. He told me he murdered a defenseless, wounded Confederate soldier to put him out of his misery. That night he hung himself in the barn. Eli and I made it look like an accident. I should have done something. I should not have left him alone. I should have stopped this. What good would the truth do for anyone now. So, I lied.

Isaac tore up the letter and threw it in the cookstove hoping his lies would burn with the paper.

May 1864
The Benjamin Miller House
Fryeburg, Maine

Dear Darian,

Thanks to your courage, Isaac and the family have a second chance at life. He has adjusted to his new wooden leg. He limps and walks with a cane, but he can do everything he did before the war. We spent the winter months working with Isaac's mother in establishing a traveling apothecary. His mother is truly an amazing woman and I am learning so much from her. Isaac knows just as much about remedies as she does. This has been a family project. Danny helped Isaac convert an old farm wagon into a peddler's wagon. The girls and David helped us package and labeled the herbs. Isaac was so excited about this new venture. I fear that David's death has devastated him and Mahayla.

Tomorrow we will be leaving for our second trip to Portland and stopping at the towns along the Pequawket Trail to sell our wares. We originally planned to leave both girls in the capable hands of Danny and Emily. However, Isaac felt that a change of scenery might lift Mahayla's spirits. I think it will be Mahayla who will be lifting Isaac's spirits.

Since David's untimely passing Isaac has become very melancholy and agitated, although he attempts to put on a brave face.

We will write you from Portland.

Yours truly
Lydia

June 1864
The Benjamin Miller House
Fryeburg, Maine

Dear Darian,

We had a successful trip to Portland and sold most of our inventory. I am looking forward to working in the gardens this summer. Mahayla is the best helper I could ask for. You will not believe how much the girls have grown. Summer is the best student at the stone schoolhouse, and she is only seven years old! She loves reading and writing stories and wants to be a teacher. Mahayla will be going to school in the fall. Although she has informed everyone that she has no intentions of ever going to school. I pity the poor teacher!

Lydia has become quite the businesswoman. I could not run this enterprise without her help.

Of course, none of this would have been possible, if you had not saved my life. I am sorry you were captured because you risked life and limb to get a letter mailed to Danny. If it was not for me, you would be a free man.

Your devoted friend,
Isaac

* * *

The general store was empty. It was the middle of haying season and the farmers were working from sunrise to sunset. Jacob wisely hired a few local boys to help on the farm for he and Eli simply could not manage the work alone. There were days that Eli came late or did not show up at all. Kate was busy with Isaac and Mahayla in the garden. Lydia completed the housework in the morning and worked on a catalog to distribute to stores. Summer assisted her mother and wrote stories in her journal.

"A letter from Georgia!"

"Go ahead and take your time. I think the boys and I can handle things here," Peter encouraged.

Rachel found Isaac in the garden and delivered the letter with a smile.

Isaac sat in the shade and read the letter in private.

Dear Isaac,

Your letters are like cups of cold water. Did you ever think that if I had not been captured, I could have been killed or wounded in the next battle? Everyone's letters give me hope that I might yet survive this war. Please thank the family for their letters. I regret I can only write an occasional letter. Please tell Danny and Emily my next letter will be for them.

The prison grows more and more overcrowded with each passing week. There is simply not enough food and clean water to go around. Tempers grow as hardships increase. There is no shelter from the hot Georgia sun or rain.[3]

Please do not mention this to Emily. You know how she worries about me. Tell Danny I have passed around some of his letters and I am even willing to go to church when I return. Please ask your mother to begin cooking as soon as the war ends because I will be mighty hungry by then.

Please keep writing.

Darian

September 1864
The Benjamin Miller House
Fryeburg, Maine

Dear Darian,

Isaac has left for another business trip. Mahayla started school last week. I made her two new dresses, but she was not impressed. Fortunately, Summer had taught her to read the primer of the McGuffey's Reader while they played school. With both girls in school I am free to help Mrs. Miller pick and dry herbs and make more remedies for Isaac's next trip.

We have not seen much of Danny and Emily for they have been very busy at the mill. I am sure they will be grateful to have you back home.

Isaac encouraged me to write to you even if I do not have much to say. We all miss you.

Yours truly,
Lydia

October 1864

Evans General Store
Fryeburg, Maine

Dear Darian,

It has been several months since your last letter arrived. What is autumn like in Georgia? The mountains here are ablaze in their fall colors and mornings and evenings are cold enough to start the stove. Isaac and Lydia are taking a new route through New Hampshire as far south as Portsmouth. We are not sure how long this trip will take them. For now, the girls are staying with us. After school Summer returns and helps me in the store and with getting supper on the table. Mahayla literally runs to the farm every afternoon, helping my mother pick, dry and garble herbs. She is learning to make some salves and package teas. I think this will soon become a three-generation family business.

Our boys are growing like weeds and prove to be a big help in the store, stocking shelves and waiting on customers.

I rarely see Eli. He sends Julia to the store to shop. She spends much time with her daughters and grandchildren. I think they are a healing balm to her soul for she appears to be doing as well as can be expected.

I am setting aside a stack of newspapers for you to read when you return home. Of course, they will be more like history books by then.

The children have returned from school. I shall bid you farewell and continue to look for your letters in the United States mail.

Holding you in our prayers,

Rachel

The Benjamin Miller House
Fryeburg, Maine
November 1864

Dear Darian,

Today was a dismal election day. Pa was having one of his spells, so he did not go to the town house to vote. I have not seen Eli in a week. Peter and I went together. He remarked that the town house felt empty with so many men away at war, dead or invalids. Of course, Rachel said if women were able to vote, there would have been plenty of people voting today. I could not argue against that. We had no family dinner.

Danny says we need to pray for both President Lincoln and George McClellan for whoever wins this election will need God's wisdom. I hear some people at the general store predicting that McClellan will win. The country has grown weary of this prolonged, bloody war and McClellan is more apt to negotiate a peace treaty with the Confederacy. That would get you home sooner. But then all those men would have died in vain.

Pa and Eli had a poor to middling harvest this year. My mother says God provides. The traveling apothecary has been successful for its first year and she has earned quite a bit of money from her share of the business. If the need should arise, she can purchase food from other farms.

Thanksgiving is coming. This year I am thankful that I can provide for my family and the girls are healthy and doing well in school. I am also thankful that you are out of harm's way and you have a home and business waiting for you to return home.

Next week, I will take off the wheels and put on the runners on the wagon and travel to Auburn through Bridgton and Naples. Does it ever snow in Georgia? We have enough snow for us to take our sleighs. Lydia thinks we should alternate the routes to compare profits. Alas, I will be traveling without the companionship of my wife. There will be too many hours leaving me alone with me thoughts.

I shall write you from Auburn.

Your friend,
Isaac

December 1864
River View Farm
Fryeburg, Maine

Dear Darian,

I promised Rachel that I would tell you President Lincoln has been reelected. I pray for that poor man. What burdens he must carry. The battles are so far away, yet we are consumed by the thoughts and sorrows of this war. Many brave Fryeburg men have been killed and wounded. There are grieving parents, widows and fatherless children.

Danny says we must dwell on our blessings and not on our losses. I have great satisfaction in the success of our traveling apothecary. I have fond memories of helping my dear grandmother in her gardens and now I have the joy of working with my own granddaughter. Lydia and Isaac have been quite successful in their business trips. There is much work to be accomplished while they are away. I am grateful to keep busy for I briefly forget David's death.

It shall be a quiet Christmas this year. Last year Rachel surprised us with a Christmas tree brightly lit with candles. I truly feared that the house would burn down. Both David and Mahayla were enthralled by the sight. I could not bear to have another tree this year, for it would simply remind me of David. Mr. Miller has been stricken with his "spells" more frequently. I fear this war has caused him much nervous agitation and distress. I do believe a large family get-together would only increase his distress.

Forgive me. These are the forlorn thoughts that come to me when I am idle. Writing to you and reading your letters bring much comfort to me. You are a strong and brave lad. You overcame much suffering and sorrow in Ireland, and I know by the grace of God you will survive your present circumstances. Remember, your family is waiting for you to come home.

Nana Miller

January 1865
Miller & Flynn Lumber Miller
Fryeburg, Maine

Dear Darian

It is a new year and I ask myself is this the year the war will end. I have been meditating on this verse from the book of James, Chapter 1, verse 12.

"Blessed is the man who perseveres under trial, because when he has stood the test, he will receive the crown of life that God has promised to those who love him."

My dearest Danny tries to protect me. He does not know that I read the newspapers and Rachel conveys the latest information on the war. I understand that prison is no better than the battlefield. Perhaps it is more severe for you are unarmed and defenseless. I know the camp is overcrowded and thousands of prisoners are dying.[4] But I beg you to persevere under your present circumstances. As trying as they must be, they are only temporary.

Please remember you have both a home in Fryeburg and an eternal home waiting for you.

Holding you in our prayers,
Emily

February 1865
Miller & Flynn Lumber Mill
Fryeburg, Maine

Dear Darian,

I have been reading in the Book of Job. Are you familiar with this story of a righteous man who had great wealth, servants and a large family? Yet the Lord allowed Job to be tested. He lost his possessions, all his children and he suffered greatly of diseased flesh. When my faith falters, I think upon Job and John Gunther.

Mr. Gunther is the owner of the farm where you brought Isaac for shelter and medical care. All his food and water were given to the troops. His crops and fields were destroyed by the fighting. His livestock escaped or were killed. His home and barn were in ruins after serving as a makeshift hospital and surgical theatre. His wife and children witnessed unspeakable horrors. He is a God-fearing man, yet he was beset by hardship.

I think upon these things and I grow ashamed of my lack of gratitude for the many blessings I enjoy. Why do the righteous suffer? Why do the innocent die? Those questions are as old as mankind. My faith is true yet untested. One can lose his home, his food, his loved ones, his leg, his life and even his liberty. But he will never lose God's infinite love.

Be strong and true in your faith for that is the very thing that the enemy cannot take from you.

Yours truly,
Danny

March 1865
River View Farm
Fryeburg, Maine

Dear Darian,

I made two brief business trips this winter. Mama slipped on the ice and is abed while she recuperates. The family has moved to the farm temporarily to run the household and to make, package and label remedies. The girls' laughter and antics appear to be good medicine. Pa has not had one of his spells for a while. He has a new audience for his old stories. To his delight Summer is writing down his stories. She says someday she will read these stories to her grandchildren. Mahayla is her grandmother's apprentice. She is practicing her penmanship and spelling by writing down a list of herbs on her slate. Lydia and I are preparing for another trip to Portland as soon as the mud dries.

We did not go out to tap trees this year. Lydia did not want to leave Mama unattended. Pa claimed he was not up to it this year. Mahayla cried and said tapping trees make her sad because she misses Davy.

Eli has all the buckets and spiels anyway. But still it does not feel right.

We have not seen Danny and Emily in weeks – but then again, we never do during mud season.

Rachel now has a crate filled with newspapers she has saved for you. When you return, your days will be filled with eating and reading. The family sends their fondest regards. Pa says the war must end soon.

Your friend,
Isaac

April 1865
Miller & Flynn Lumber Mill
Fryeburg, Maine

Dear Darian,

I grow more anxious for you by the day. It has been over eight months since your last letter. Danny says I am worried about nothing and when we are finally able to get to town, there will be a few letters from you waiting for us. I pray that he is right. When you return, I wish to hear about the other men in your camp. I am sure they have families anxiously awaiting their return as we are. Every soldier has a story.
I must begin supper. I will finish this letter tomorrow.

Emily never finished the letter.

XX

War's End

On the morning of April 10, 1865 Rachel rushed into her parents' kitchen where she found all three of her brothers and her parents.

She placed a copy of the newspaper on the table. "It is over! The war ended yesterday! Robert E. Lee surrendered the last major Confederate army to Ulysses S. Grant at Appomattox Court House on April 9." [1]

"Where is the courthouse?" Eli asked.

"Appomattox Court House is the name of a town in Virginia. Some of the towns which are the county seat are called Court House," Isaac explained. "Like South Paris is the county seat of Oxford County."

"So, Lee did not surrender in a courthouse?" Jacob asked.

"The newspaper says the surrender occurred in the parlor of the home of Wilmer McLean." [2]

"Thank God this nightmare is over," Jacob breathed a sigh of relief.

"The nightmare of war and slavery are both over," Daniel added as he abruptly stood up. "I must tell Emily! Darian will be coming home soon!" he ran out the door.

"All of us will have supper tonight to celebrate!" Kate announced.

Eli silently left the house and headed to the barn. "I will go talk to him," Isaac offered as he grabbed his cane and followed his brother.

"Will David be celebrating tonight? Will Monroe be celebrating? I have nothing to celebrate. Go away, Isaac."

"I understand."

"You do not understand!" Eli raged. "No one understands! He did not die a hero in battle like Monroe. He died a coward."

"He was no coward! You are the one who does not understand! You eat three meals a day, you do not understand what it is like to go hungry day and night. You sleep in your bed every night. You do not understand what it is like to spend countless nights cold, wet, sick and hungry! You do not know what it is like to wipe someone's brains off your face. Or to hear a man's screams. Or to have men die in your arms. Or try to wash the blood off your uniform. You do not understand the deafening, bone rattling thunder of cannons. Or to have your eyes burn from the smoke of a thousand rifles. You understand nothing!

David was no coward. The pain in his soul was as real as the pain in my leg. Try to be a man and do not begrudge Danny and Emily's joy in Darian's return."

"Get out! Get out!" Eli screamed.

"David was a real hero. Every day he faced his fears. You cannot face your son's suicide. You are the coward!"

"Get out!

* * *

No one acknowledged Eli and Julia's absence at supper that night.

"We shall have a supper like this when Darian returns," Emily beamed with excitement.

"When will he be returning?" Lydia asked.

"I guess we will receive a letter from the army or somebody official," Daniel replied with uncertainty.

"I will take a ship to Georgia and get him myself, if I have to!" Emily declared.

"A lady cannot take a trip like that alone. We will all go together!" Jacob proclaimed.

* * *

As Peter placed a stack of newspapers on the counter, he stared at the frontpage headlines.

"A letter from Georgia for Danny and Emily!" Rachel waved the envelope. Before Peter had the opportunity to respond, Rachel had put on her shawl and bonnet and ran out the door.

She burst into her parents' kitchen. "Isaac! I have a letter for Danny from Georgia!" She panted.

"Mercy! Did you run all the way here?" Kate asked.

"Isaac, take it to the mill to Danny and Emily. I have to get back to the store."

Isaac tried to conceal his excitement for Eli's benefit when he entered the barn. "Pa, I need to go out to the mill. Danny has a letter from Georgia."

Eli turned away as Jacob smiled but said nothing.

* * *

Rachel felt like skipping back to the store. Her joy was short lived as Peter greeted her at the door.

"President Lincoln has been shot." He quietly stated.

"What! How? No! That is impossible!"

He silently handed her the newspaper.

Lincoln Shot at Ford Theater
No Hope for Recovery!

"Peter, what will happen?"

"Only God knows."

The two sat silently in shock and despair.

* * *

"Emily! Emily!" Isaac knocked on the kitchen door before letting himself in.

"Isaac, what a surprise. Is anything wrong?"

"Everything is right," he grinned as he handed her the letter.

She eagerly tore open the envelope and began to read. Her hands trembled, her face paled, she screamed, and fell to the floor. "Why? Why, God? Why?" she sobbed hysterically.

Isaac picked up the letter.

Dear Mr. & Mrs. Miller,

It is with my deepest regrets that I must inform you of the passing of Darian Flynn on April 9, 1865 at Andersonville Prison where he succumbed to the hardships and deprivations of prison life...

Daniel came running in the house upon hearing his wife's screams.

"I am sorry, Danny. I am so sorry," he whispered as he handed his brother the letter.

Daniel wordlessly slumped to the floor, held his wife in his arms and choked back sobs.

"How could God do this to us?" Emily demanded. "He sent Darian to be the son we never had. Why would He then take him away? Why did he have to die the day the war ended? What kind of a cruel joke is that? Why did God let our son die in a filthy prison camp?"

"Do not blame the Lord for the sins of man. Let us thank Him for the eighteen months we had to share our love with him. Mr. and Mrs. Quint did not have that opportunity.

Let us treasure the few letters we have from him. Let us rejoice that Darian understood and received his Savior's redeeming love. Though we are in pain for a time, we can anticipate the future we will share in Eternity with Darian."

"Why? Danny, why?"

"I know the Lord has a reason. But we may never know it this side of heaven."

"Danny, is there anything I can do?" Isaac timidly asked.

Daniel helped his wife to her feet and to a chair. "Kindly tell the family that we shall not be in church on Sunday. Please ask them for their prayers and to respect our privacy. We will come to the farm when we are ready."

"You know Rachel will come as soon as she learns of this," Isaac warned.

Daniel nodded, "We have indeed been blessed with a loving sister."

"You mean stubborn."

"Please ask Rachel to respect my wishes."

"He saved my life, Danny. I would have died in that wheat field if it was not for him. Lydia would be a widow and my girls would be fatherless."

Daniel put his hand on Isaac's shoulder. "You were Darian's most faithful friend from the day he arrived in Fryeburg. For that I shall always be grateful. Now go home and mourn the loss of your best friend while Emily and I mourn the loss of our son."

Blinded by tears, Isaac limped to the awaiting horse. He wrapped his arms around the patient animal's neck, buried his face into her mane and cried. "Why? Why am I the only one of the four of us to survive? What is the purpose of all this suffering? Why am I still here? Lord, if you hear me, tell me why!"

* * *

Isaac found Eli in the field. "Where is Pa?"

"He is resting. Do not bother him," he muttered without turning around.

"Good. You are the one I came to talk to."

"Whatever for!" He quickly turned and faced his brother. "What do you need now?"

"Darian is dead!"

Eli cursed under his breath and looked away.

"Eli, everyone knows your Pa's favorite. You are the one the family depends on. You are right. I have been lazy and shiftless, and it has not been fair to you or Pa and Lydia. I am trying, Eli, I really am. But I need you to tell Pa. I thought Davy's death was going to kill him, but he held out hope that Darian would someday return. I need you to tell Pa. He will take it better if you tell him."

Eli sighed as he nervously ran his hand through his hair. "Ma is at the general store. You tell the ladies while I go talk to Pa." He slowly headed to the house.

* * *

The bell over the door rang as Isaac entered the busy store. He found Peter at the counter selling newspapers

"Is my mother here?"

"Have you read the newspaper today?" Peter asked holding up a copy.

"Of course not. Why?"

"Lincoln has been shot," Mr. Weston explained

"Yes. She and Lydia are with Rachel upstairs to plan a welcome home dinner. But I think they intend to defer the planning to another day.

Isaac's shoulders slumped.

"Isaac, what is it? What is wrong? Oh, no! Do not tell me that…"

"I need to talk to my mother first."

He found the ladies talking seriously and sipping tea.

"Isaac, did you hear the terrible news?" Rachel asked.

"Yeah. Peter told me."

"Next week we will plan a celebration for Darian. It does not seem proper to do it today," Kate explained.

"Mama, I fear there will be no celebration for this family."

Kate dropped her teacup and it smashed on the floor. She stood up, "Are you telling us that…"

"Darian is dead," Isaac blurted.

"Poor Emily! We must go to her!" Lydia instructed.

"I will get the wagon. All three of us will go," Rachel proposed.

"No! Danny requested that we give them time and privacy while they grieve. They will come to us when they are ready," Isaac explained.

"But surely…" Rachel began.

"Danny was quite explicit. No visitors. He was adamant that the family respect their privacy, Rachel. I know that you mean well, but your presence will not help," Isaac defied his sister. "Mama, Eli is telling Papa now. I fear this may cause one of his spells. Let me take you home."

"Of course," Kate said in a daze. "Are you sure he is really dead? Maybe they made a mistake."

"I am sorry, Mama. It is no mistake. Darian is dead."

"Lydia, would you care to remain here for a while? I think Rachel would appreciate your company. You and I will tell the girls together this afternoon." Isaac took his mother's arm and escorted her back to the farm.

* * *

It was not easy, but the family restrained itself from visiting Daniel and Emily. While the nation mourned the death of an American President, the Millers mourned the loss of an Irish orphan.

Three weeks later Daniel and Emily entered the general store. "Oh Danny," Rachel threw her arms around her brother and wept. "Emily, how are you doing?" she took her sister-in-law's hands.

"I am doing better. Thank you," she bravely responded.

"Could you join us at the farm?" Daniel invited.

"Take as long as you need, Rachel. I will run the store," Peter offered. "Danny, we are so sorry for your loss," he shook his brother-in-law's hand. "The entire town is in shock and mourning."

"Thank you for your kindness," Daniel replied swallowing the lump in his throat.

"Emily dear," Kate greeted her daughter-in-law as she, Danny and Rachel entered the kitchen. "What may we do for you? Please stay for supper. Oh, Danny. I have lost another grandson!" she cried.

"We shall continue on," Daniel quietly responded.

"Danny, I am so sorry," Eli solemnly shook his hand.

"I know you are, and I thank you for it. Isaac, I know. You need not say a word. Pa, may we sit down, there are some things we need to discuss with the family."

Lydia and the girls arrived. "Oh Emily!" she ran to hug her. "I saw you and Danny pass the window and we had to come see you!"

"Aunt Emily," Mahayla cried and held fast to her aunt's skirt. "I am too sad!"

"I am too sad as well," she put her arms around her nieces. "But seeing you again helps me to feel better."

"Please everyone, take a seat at the table," Jacob invited. "Danny wishes to speak to us." Turning to his granddaughters, "You may go upstairs and play with some of Aunt Rachel's dolls and do not interrupt the grownups."

"Son, I feel so helpless."

Daniel cleared his throat. "I have sold the lumber mill, our home and all the timberland at a fair price. My small mill cannot compete with the large logging operations up north. I cannot continue running the mill alone, even if I could find hired help. There are few able-bodied young men who wish to remain in Fryeburg."

The family sat in stunned silence before Kate asked, "Where will you live?"

"Pa, I would like to purchase an acre of land from you and build a house. This way I may help on the farm during haying and harvest. I understand I could never replace the work that David and Isaac could provide, but perhaps I may be of some service."

"I will give you as much land as you need."

"To think of having all of my children nearby!" Kate patted Daniel's arm.

"Oh Emily, the girls and I will love having you live just down the road! You can come over for tea and…" Lydia was too excited for words.

Emily smiled. "Nothing would make me happier than to see the girls every day."

Daniel continued, "By living in the village, Emily and I will have more opportunities to serve the church than if we remained isolated at Walker's Falls at the mill.

Isaac, you are not the same man you were before you left for war. I have seen your care and compassion for the suffering. I am amazed at your knowledge of herbs and remedies. I watched your enthusiasm as you help Ma in the herb garden and prepare salves and tinctures.

I know you have questioned, why did you survive when your three friends did not."

Isaac remained silent.

"Emily and I decided that with a portion of the proceeds, we would like to pay your expenses to go to Bowdoin Medical School and become a doctor." [4]

"How did you know? How did you know that I want to become a doctor?" Isaac demanded. He told no one, not even Lydia.

Daniel replied. "Is it not obvious? Ma taught you about medicine. The battlefield taught you compassion. You survived so you may help others to survive. You suffered so you may alleviate the suffering of others."

"There are two conditions to this offer," Emily began.

"I will pay you back," Isaac offered.

"That is not one of the conditions," Emily disagreed. "The first, we may live in your house while we are building ours. The second, you must return to Fryeburg and open your medical practice in your grandfather's office."

"It is with much humility and gratitude that I accept your generous offer. I do wish to become a doctor!"

"Your grandfather would be so proud," Jacob nodded his approval.

"I hope I will be a better doctor than a farmer!"

For the first time in a year, Eli laughed.

XXI

The Reason

It was July of 1867 when Daniel and Emily sat in the front parlor of Isaac's home. "Emily, I thought you would be happy with the new house."

"Danny, it will be a beautiful home. I just think that it will be much too large for the two of us."

"This house is not for the two of us. I trust the Lord has plenty of people who will need shelter and a home from time to time. There are students who would like to attend Fryeburg Academy, but who live too far away. We will have a home filled with energetic and enthusiastic young people. There are elderly people who do not have children to care for them and cannot live alone."

"Well, now the house is not big enough!" she laughed.

There was a knock on the kitchen door. "Hello! Hello!" Kate called excitedly.

Daniel ran to the kitchen to greet his parents. "Have you received a letter from Isaac?"

"We have a new grandson!" Kate announced. "We are here to celebrate. Emily, put the tea on and I have a pie!"

"His name is Benjamin Charles Miller and he was born on my father's one hundredth birthday! He will be called Charlie because there can only be one Benjamin Miller," Jacob explained. "The Lord has given me a grandson in my old age. Not that Charlie could ever replace David or Darian."

"I understand, Pa. There is a time to mourn and a time to rejoice. Today we shall rejoice!" Daniel was thankful that his father had not experienced one of his spells in almost a year.

The family gathered around the dining room table as Emily poured the tea and Kate served the pie. "I remember the day my mother bought these dishes," Jacob reminisced. "Darian smashed all of her old dishes. The poor boy. It is a terrible thing when grief turns to anger and mourning turns to rage.

He lost his entire family, his parents, grandparents, brothers, sisters back in Ireland. It was a privilege to be Darian's family. When I feel sorry for myself for losing two grandsons, I think of the courage Darian had to continue his life after so much loss."

The conversation was interrupted by a knock on the front door. "Who can that be? No one ever comes to the front door," Emily mused.

"Whoever it is, we may offer them tea and pie," Kate went to the hutch to retrieve more teacups, saucers, plates and silverware.

Daniel found a thin, pale young man coughing into a cotton handkerchief. He looked uncomfortable in his new suit.

"Excuse me, sir," he pulled at his stiff white collar. "I am lookin for Mr. Daniel Miller. The nice lady at the general store told me that I would find him at this address." He nervously inhaled and continued as if he had memorized a speech. "I do hope I am not disturbin you."

"I am Daniel Miller and the nice lady at the general store is my sister. How may I help you?"

"Sir, my name is Josiah Greene and my wife thought I should – I mean I am – I was a friend of Darian Flynn. My wife thought I should visit you and tell you about his last days."

"Do come in," Emily invited.

"Please join us for tea and pie," Kate continued.

"I do not mean to be a bother, mam," he looked around the house nervously.

"Have a seat, son," Jacob pulled out a chair. "Any friend of Darian's is a friend of ours."

The young man sat down wearily and placed a small, canvas sack under the table. "Thank you, sir. I cannot stay long for I must catch the stagecoach back to Portland. This pie is delicious. I would have come sooner, but I have been feelin poorly." He stifled a cough into his handkerchief.

"Were you in the 17th Maine?" Daniel asked.

"No, sir. We met in Andersonville prison. I thought battle was hell until the day I found myself in that prison camp. We lived practically out in the open in make-shift shanties of scrap wood and blankets. At first there was a creek of fresh flowing water, but it soon became a pool of filth. The creek became a swamp. There was never enough to eat. As the prison grew more crowded, violence erupted between groups of prisoners. People would steal your food and ..."

Daniel interrupted for he wanted to spare Emily. "We are sorry for your suffering. Darian alluded to the vile conditions in his letters."

"Yes, sir. I do not like to discuss those days. But my wife says there are things I should tell you that may bring you comfort."

"Please continue," Emily anxiously encouraged.

"I do not reckon I remember the day I met him. Every day was just like the rest. He was worried something fierce about a letter he wrote. He was ambushed in Gettysburg right after he left a man's house. He hoped that the man was able to get that letter mailed because he was worried about his friend."

"That friend is my brother. By the grace of God, we received the letter," Daniel assured.

"Well we found out that his friend was alive a year later when your letter came. But back then he didn't know nothin. I thought living in a regular army camp was bad. It was like a palace compared to this place. Them rebels treated us like animals.

Darian told us that the rebels ain't so bad. Not compared to the British and what they did to all those starvin Irish. I lost my pa when I was fifteen. Can't imagine losin everybody! Boy, could he spin a yarn. We would all sit around and listen to him talk about Ireland and rottin potatoes and diggin graves and he was just a young lad. He told us all about Saint Patrick. Boy I could just imagine old Saint

Pat drivin out the snakes. It was like bein right with him in Ireland. It made a man forget his miseries for a piece."

"Mr. Greene, would you care for another piece of pie?" Kate offered.

"Don't mind if I do. I mean, thank you, mam if it ain't too much trouble," he handed her his plate. "Could I have another cup of tea to wash it down with?"

"Darian was a good storyteller," Daniel agreed.

"Darn good storyteller. The way he described this house. It looks just like he said," he looked around. "I am sorry that I cannot meet Senator Miller and his wife them bein dead and all. Is it true what Darian said?"

"What did Darian say?" Kate asked.

"About the secret tunnel in this house and sneakin out runaway slaves and all."

"It is not a secret now. But yes, it is true," Jacob assured.

"Your grandmother was one of those Quakers?"

"Yes, she was. I think we want to hear about Darian and not about our family."

"Well, Darian was such a good storyteller, it made us forget. Then the other men would tell stories about their families. There were Swedish farmers from the Midwest, Jewish merchants from New York, Irish laborers from Boston, German farmers from Pennsylvania. One man's grandfather helped build the Erie Canal. Another man's father worked on the railroad. It makes you proud to be an American. You know different religions, the different nationalities, the different accents. We never had no slaves. We all worked for what we had. Darian made us feel good about ourselves.

You know some of us use to call him Doc."

"Really? Why?" Emily asked.

"Some of us would get sick, and he would be out there pickin weeds and makin us tea. By golly, didn't we get better. Most of us. Some men died anyway, but it weren't Darian's fault. Them men were too far gone."

Kate smiled with satisfaction.

"Don't you know one night one of them guards wakes him up demanding some medicine tea. Darian gives him some. No way would I have done that. I would have poisoned that son of – Excuse me, mam. Darian said, that ain't Christian like. Good thing too. That tea was for the guard's daughter, not for him. I would have felt mighty bad if I poisoned a little girl. I have three little girls of my own. Well only two back then.

The day we could write letters, boy that was a happy day. Darian helped me write a letter to my wife and mother. I don't have much learnin. My minister would read my letters to them and then write down their words back to me.

It was like Christmas when one of your letters arrived. Some of us called him the preacher. He would read your letters – the religious parts at least to us. One night the guard with the sick daughter gave Darian a New Testament with Psalms. He would read from that book and explain real good what those words meant. We even had a baptism. He sprinkled a few men with water. Heck, nobody would dare go in that filthy stream. He would read The Lord is My Shepherd psalm at funerals. When some men were dyin, they would want Darian to come to pray for them.

It is a mighty fearful thing when a man gives up hope. He gave us hope. This too shall pass, he would tell us. We will get out of here one way or the other. We will either go home to our families or Home to our Savior."

"More tea?" Kate asked.

"No thank you, mam. I need to catch the stagecoach back home."

"Before I forget, my wife says I should give you these." He handed Daniel the sack.

"These are our letters! He kept all of our letters?"

"Yes, sir. Just before he died, he gave them all to me. To give me hope, he says. I read some of the good ones – best I could - every day. It eases my mind because ..." he stopped and stared out the window. "He's dead because of me. I was mighty sick – mighty sick with camp cough. He made me tea, a poultice. He told me I had to eat to keep my strength. The war was almost over. He kept tellin me to hold on. I would be home to my wife and little girls real soon.

He gave me his food. He gave me his rations. He was starvin so he could give me his food. He gave me his letters. He died so I could live and go home to my family." He tightly shut his eyes.

"I'm mighty sorry. I am the reason Darian died. I am the reason."

"No, Josiah," Daniel contradicted. "You are not the reason Darian died. Darian is the reason you are alive."

"You said you have a new daughter?" Emily asked.

"Yes, mam," he wiped his tears with his sleeve.

"What is her name?"

"Dari Anne"

Daniel and Emily looked at one another. The Reason.

Discussion Questions

I Election Day

1. How was the election of 1860 different from the previous elections?
2. Name the political parties involved. How were they created?
3. What previous parties no longer existed in 1860?
4. How was election day in Fryeburg in 1860 different from the elections in your town today?

II Snowstorms and Headlines

1. How did Fryeburg and the Millers receive the news? Compare and contrast to today's news media.
2. List some of the events which were in the news.
3. How did the town's people react?
4. How did the news impact the lives of the town's people?

III Declaration of War

1. What event started the war? Where did it take place? Who made the first move?
2. Why did the Millers believe it would be a short war? How did life in the North differ from life in the South?
3. Why did Jacob ask his son Daniel to take over writing the Fryeburg Chronicles? Do you agree with Jacob's reasons? Explain your answer.
4. Why was Thaddeus Pierce in Washington?

5. How did some of the residents of Washington respond to the first battle?
6. Where did it take place?
7. Who won?

IV Enlistment

1. What are sharpshooters? How did they get their name?
2. What are the qualifications for sharpshooters?
3. Why did Darian enlist?
4. What were some of Darian's experiences? How did he respond?
5. State the reasons why David, Monroe and Isaac enlisted in the 17th Regiment of Maine.
6. What experiences did these three traveling to Washington?

V The Home Front

1. Why did Daniel and Emily move in with Lydia?
2. List some of Lydia's struggles? What do you think is the root of these struggles?
3. Describe Summer's first day of school? How did this compare to your first day?
4. What changes in Lydia do you observe? What is her motivation for these changes?

VI The Schaeffer Family

1. We often read about the soldiers on the battlefields. Have you ever imagined what it would be like to be a civilian?
2. What adjectives would you use to describe Mrs. Schaeffer?
3. What do you think happened to David on the battlefield? How would you describe his behavior?

VII The Gunther Family

1. What was the last few days in June 1863 like for Joseph and Emma Gunther?
2. What choices did Mr. Gunther make on July 1?
3. What happened to Gunther's Mercantile?
4. Describe John Gunther's farm before the battle.
5. Describe the horrors and sacrifices this family experienced.
6. Where did they treat the wounded?
7. How did young Henry Gunther respond to these events?
8. Darian left his post to save Isaac's life. Do you agree or disagree with his actions?

VIII The Reporter

1. Why did Thaddeus Pierce travel to Gettysburg the day after the battle? What was he planning to report on? How did he finally arrive?
2. Who was Dr. Letterman?
3. What did the reporter find when he arrived?
4. Where were the wounded being treated? Why?
5. Why did most of the army doctors leave their patients?
6. Why was there a great need for shovels?
7. What were some of the locations the reporter visited?

IX The Arrival

1. Why did Daniel leave for Gettysburg? Describe his trip.
2. What anxieties did he have?
3. What did he see and experience at the train depot?
4. How did the Gunther family respond to Daniel's visit?

X The Search

1. What does Daniel do when he discovers that Isaac is no longer in the Gunther's barn?

2. Why does he visit the U.S. Christian Commission first? What does he find there?
3. What does he find at St. Francis Xavier Catholic Church? What civilians are there? Why does he stay there after he learns that Isaac is not there?
4. Christ Lutheran Church was the first building commandeered as a hospital. How did this Union hospital fall behind enemy lines?
5. How does Daniel help at the Lutheran Church?

XI Camp Letterman

1. Describe Camp Letterman. Where was it located? How large was it? What services did it provide?
2. Daniel finally finds Isaac. What condition is he in?
3. What was the issue with the soldier in the next cot? Do you think this set up was a wise decision by the army?
4. How has Daniel changed during the weeks he spent in Gettysburg?

XII The Return

1. How did each family member react to Isaac's return?
2. What changes did he find?
3. What did he learn about Darian, David and Monroe?

XIII A Long Row to Hoe

1. How did Isaac compensate for his amputation?
2. How was Eli coping with the uncertainty of David's fate?
3. Tensions explode when Eli and Isaac get into a fight. What does Jacob tell Isaac? Is it ever acceptable to break a promise or betray a secret?
4. What does Jacob tell Eli?
5. How did the war impact Fryeburg Academy and the Fryeburg Fair?

XIV A New Beginning

1. Describe Kate's catalog purchase.
2. What is Kate's plan?
3. How does this new enterprise draw the family closer together?

XV Discovery in Gettysburg

1. Why did Thaddeus return to Gettysburg?
2. What was his response to the rumors of the ghost?
3. What were people's response to Lincoln's brief speech?
4. How did the soldier respond to Thaddeus' offer of food and friendship?

XVI A Tale of Two Homecomings

1. Compare how various family members responded to Thaddeus' and David's homecoming.
2. Do you think David is a deserter? Support your answer.
3. How has the Miller family been deceiving people for four generations? What was your response to Isaac forging David's discharge papers?

XVII The Adjustments

1. How did David adjust to civilian life? How did various family members respond to his struggles?
2. How is he relating to the family?
3. What Christmas surprise was waiting for the Miller

XVIII Secrets

1. After saving his grandfather's life, how does David respond to the events? Why?
2. David reveals a secret to Isaac. How does Isaac respond? How would you respond?

3. Why does Isaac agree to cover up David's suicide? He says, "It is too late for the truth." Do you agree or disagree with this statement?

XIX Andersonville Prison Letters

1. How did the family learn of Darian's imprisonment?
2. Why were the prisoners in Libby Prison moved to Georgia?
3. How does Daniel try to encourage Darian in his letters?
4. What do you learn about Andersonville through Darian's letters?
5. What do you learn about Isaac's new business through his letters?

XX War's End

1. What two awful events do the Millers learn of on the same day?
2. How has Isaac change since his return from the war?
3. What life changes have Daniel and Emily made?
4. Contrast Daniel's and Eli's reactions to the uncertainty of their sons' fate and to the reality of their sons' deaths.
5. How do you explain the difference?

XXI The Reason

1. What special event happened to the Miller family?
2. What impact did Darian's imprisonment and death have on his fellow inmates?
3. What was the reason for Darian's death? Can God turn a tragedy into a victory?

Fryeburg Landmarks

Fryeburg Academy

Founded in 1792, Fryeburg Academy is one of the oldest private schools in the United States serving a diverse population of local and boarding students from around the country and the world.

1913 photo of Fryeburg Academy built in brick after the wooden structure burned to the ground in 1851.

Photo courtesy of Fryeburg Historical Society.

Village School House

This stone building served as the Village School House for many decades.

Today it serves as the Fryeburg Public Library

Photo courtesy of Fryeburg Historical Society.

Fryeburg Town House

The town house was constructed in 1847 and was used for over 100 years for town meetings and voting.

Today it is the home of the Currier Doll Museum where a few wooden voting booths remain.

Photo courtesy of the Fryeburg Historical Society.

First Congregational Church of Fryeburg

In 1775 Rev. Fessenden answered the call to pastor the church in a meeting house, located in Center Fryeburg. In 1795 a second meeting house was built in the Village to accommodate the growing population and served until 1850.

A new church building on Main Street was dedicated in 1850 and still serves as a house of worship today.

Photo courtesy of the Fryeburg Historical Society.

The Oxford Hotel

It has been part of Fryeburg since James and Abigail Osgood rented out rooms in their Main Street home in the late 1700's.

Over the decades the property expanded several times until it burned in 1887.

An undated photo taken before 1887 Courtesy of the Fryeburg Historical Society

The Judah Dana House

This home was built in 1816 by Senator Judah Dana on the corner of Main and River Streets.

When it was torn down in 1956 to build the Fryeburg Post office, they discovered a granite lined tunnel that went under the street. According to oral tradition, this home was part of the underground railroad.

This is the location and description of the fictional Senator Benjamin Miller Home.

Courtesy of the Fryeburg Historical Society

Book V

Fryeburg Men Serving in the 17th Regiment of Maine

Webster Barker
Frank C. Charles
Moses L. Charles
Enoch S. Chase
James G. Holt
William M. Jenkins
Patrick Lawless
Augustus F. Long
Sidney G. Morton
William B. Morton
Monroe Quint
Albion Richardson
Daniel Smith, Jr.
Ivory F. Snow
John L. Stanley
Samuel C. Stanley
Alfred E. Thompson
Alden B. Walker
John S. Walker
Joseph C. Walker
Joseph Wiley

The Fryeburg Chronicles
Own the Entire Series

Book I *The Amazing Grace* (1781-1784)

Meet the fictional Miller family, early settlers of Fryeburg, Maine as they use their Yankee ingenuity to survive the challenges of rural farm life during the Revolutionary War.

Points of Interest:

American Revolution	Herbal Medicine
Architecture	Period Clothing
Basket Weaving	Period Furniture
Cooking on a Hearth	Recipes
Dyeing Wool	Spinning
Farming	Timber Framing
Geometry	Weaving

Book II *A Secret and a Promise* (1792-1806)

Now in their 20's, the Miller brothers are beginning new careers, marrying and having families in a new nation. Attorney Benjamin Miller becomes the first preceptor of Fryeburg Academy.

Points of Interest:

Constitutional Convention	Cabinet Making
Founding of Washington D.C.	Making Paints
Louisiana Purchase	Sewing Quilts
New Monetary System	Making Soap
Shays Rebellion	Recipes
Building a Birch Bark Canoe	Rug Hooking
Building a Cider Press	Williamsburg, VA

Book III *Portraits of Change* (1819-1828)

The Miller family continues with their involvement in the Underground Railroad. Senator Benjamin Miller moves to Washington, D.C. to represent the new state of Maine.

Points of Interest:

Whale Oil Lamps	Panic of 1819
Noah Webster	Washington Irving
Maine Statehood	The Erie Canal
Missouri Compromise	Herbal Remedies
The Election of 1824	Washington, D.C.
The Underground Railroad	

Book IV *Journeys From Home* (1848-1853)

The nation and the Miller family become more divided. Benjamin's granddaughter leaves Fryeburg to work in a textile mill. A grandson, who is a newspaper reporter, brings home an Irish orphan and some new ideas.

Points of Interest:

The Irish Potato Famine	St. Patrick
The Rise of Textile Mills	1849 Gold Rush
The Free Soil Party	Moby Dick
The Communist Manifesto	Karl Marx
The Last of the Mohicans	James Fenimore Cooper

End Notes

I
Election Day

1. Paul Johnson, <u>A History of the American People</u> (New York, HarperCollins, 1997) pg. 449
2. Johnson pg. 442
3. Johnson pg. 441

II
Snowstorms and Headlines

1. Dennis and Peter Gaffney, <u>The Seven Day Scholar</u> (New York, Hyperion, 2011) pg. 31
2. Ibid
3. Ibid
4. www.history.com/this-day-in-history/jefferson-davis-elected-confederate-president

III
War!

1. www.wikipedia.org.wikiorigins_of_the_civil_war
2. Gaffney pg. 57
3. Ibid
4. Johnson pg. 455
5. Ibid
6. www.mainememory.net/sitebuilder/site/2558
7. Gaffney pg. 62
8. www.learningherbs.com/remedies-recipes/dandelion-fritters
9. Gaffney pg. 65
10. Ibid
11. www.wikipedia.org/wiki/washington-D.C._in_the_American_Civil_War_ George_ Templeton_ Strong
12. Gaffney pg. 73

13. www.civilwar.org/learn/civilwar/battle-bull-run-fact-summary
14. Gaffney pg. 75-76

IV
Enlistment

1. www.berdansharpshooters.org/history
2. Ibid
3. Ibid
4. Ibid
5. Gaffney, pg. 202

V
The Home Front

1. Lydia Childs, The American Frugal Housewife, (Boston, Carter, Hendee, and Co., 1833) pg.1

VI
The Schaeffer Family

1. Gerald R. Bennett, Days of Uncertainty and Dread, (Gettysburg Foundation, 2008) pgs. 1-3
2. Bennett, pgs. 10-15
3. Bennett, pgs. 17-19
4. Bennett, pg. 60

VII
The Gunther Family

1. Bennett, pg. 5,7
2. Bennet, pg. 20
3. Tillie Pierce Aleman, At Gettysburg, What a Girl Saw and Heard of the Battle (New York, 1889. Reprinted and distributed Stan Clark Military Books, Gettysburg, 1994) pg. 41-42
4. Frank R. Freemon, Gangrene and Glory (University of Illinois Press, 1998) pg. 48, 232
5. Freemon, pg. 109
6. Nancie W. Gudmestad, The Shrivers' Story Eyewitness to the Battle of Gettysburg (Gettysburg, Shriver House Museum, 2008) pg. 53

7. Gudmestad, pg. 49
8. www.mainememorynetwork.org
9. Bennett, pg. 68
10. Bennett, pg. 70

VIII
The Reporter

1. Gerard A. Patterson, <u>The Debris of Battle,</u> (Mechanicsburg, PA, Stackpole Books, 1997) pgs. 8-9
2. Patterson, pg. 3-4
3. Patterson, pg. 4
4. Gudmestad, pgs. 71-72
5. Gudmestad, pg. 73
6. Patterson, pg. 3
7. Patterson, pg. 4
8. Patterson, pg. 10
9. Daniel J. Hoisington, <u>Gettysburg and the Christian Commission</u> (Edinborough Press, 2002) Pg. 13
10. Hoisington, pg. 14
11. Patterson, pg. 20
12. Patterson, pg. 21
13. Patterson, pg. 14
14. Patterson, pg. 3
15. Patterson, pg. 21

IX
The Arrival

1. Alleman, pg. 101
2. Patterson, pg. 122

X
The Search

1. www.stfrancisxavier.org/hospital
2. Hoisington, pg. 13
3. Hoisington, pg. 16
4. Hoisington, pg. 14
5. www.stfrancisxavier.org/hospital

6. Ibid
7. Ibid
8. Ibid
9. www.hymnsite.com The United Methodist Hymnal Number 357. Text by Charlotte Elliot
10. Patterson, pg. 25
11. A Sanctuary for the Wounded: The Civil War Hospital at Christ Lutheran Church, (Gettysburg, PA. Christ Evangelical Lutheran Church. 2009.) pg. 3
12. pg. 28 Fryeburg Fair Book Committee,
13. pg.31
14. pg.28

XI
Camp Letterman

1. Patterson, pg.151
2. Patterson, pg. 154-155
3. Patterson, pg. 132

XIII
A Long Row to Hoe

1. John S. Barrows, Fryeburg An Historical Sketch, (Pequawket Press, 1938) pg. 128
2. Fryeburg Fair Book Committee, Fryeburg Fair First 150 years 1851-2000, 2000 pg. 24
3. Fryeburg Fair Book Committee, pg. 28
4. Fryeburg Fair Book Committee, pg. 29
5. Fryeburg Fair Book Committee, pg. 25

XIV
A New Beginning

1. www.civilwarmed.org/prosthetics
2. Ibid
3. Nancy Ondra, The A-Z Guide to Herbs that Heal (Rodale Press, 1995) pg. 18
4. Ondra, pg. 31
5. Ondra, pg. 19
6. Ibid

XV
Discovery at Gettysburg

1. www.abrahamlincolnonline.org/lincoln/site/gettysburg
2. Ibid
3. Ibid
4. Ibid
5. Ibid
6. Ibid
7. www.abrahamlincolnonline.org/lincoln/speech/gettysburg
8. www.abrahamlincolnonline.org/lincoln/site/gettysburg
9. Ibid
10. Psalm 23 King James Version

XVI
A Tale of Two Homecomings

1. www.thepeopleshistory.com
2. www.mainememorynetwork.org

XVII
The Adjustments

1. www.whychristmas.com/customs/trees.shtml
2. Ibid

XIX
The Andersonville Letters

1. Gudmestad, pgs.81-81
2. Ibid
3. Ibid
4. Gudmestad, pg.83

XX
War's End

1. Gaffney, pg. 40
2. www.library.bowdoin.edu/arch/archives/msmg.shtml

Bibliography

Adams, Michael C. <u>Living Hell: The Dark Side of the Civil War.</u> Baltimore. John Hopkins University Press. 2014.

Alleman, Pierce, Tillie. <u>At Gettysburg, or What a Girl Saw and Heard of the Battle.</u> New York. 1889. Reprinted and Distributed by Butternut and Blue, Baltimore, MD and Stan Clark Military Books in Gettysburg, PA 1994.

Barrows, John Stuart. <u>Fryeburg An Historical Sketch.</u> Fryeburg, Maine. Pequawket Press. 1938

Bennett, Gerald R. <u>Days of "Uncertainty and Dread": The Ordeal Endured by the Citizens at Gettysburg.</u> Gettysburg, PA. the Gettysburg Foundation. 2008.

Childs, Lydia. <u>The American Frugal Housewife.</u> Boston, Carter, Hendee and Co. 1833

Freemon, Frank R. <u>Gangrene and Glory.</u> University of Illinois Press. 1998

Fryeburg Fair Book Committee. <u>The Fryeburg Fair: First 150 Years.</u> Fryeburg, Maine. 2000

Gaffney, Dennis and Gaffney Peter. <u>The Seven Day Scholar: Exploring History One Week at a Time, The Civil War.</u> New York. Hyperion. 2011.

Gudemestad, Nancie W. <u>The Shrivers' Story: Eyewitnesses to the Battle of Gettysburg.</u> Gettysburg, PA. The Shriver House Museum 2013.

Hoisington, Daniel J. <u>Gettysburg and the Christian Commission.</u> Edinborough Press. 2002.

Johnson, Paul. <u>A History of the American People.</u> New York. HarperCollins. 1997

Ondra, Nancy, compiled and edited. <u>The A-Z Guide to Herbs That Heal.</u> Emmaus, Pa. Rodale Press. 1995

Patterson, Gerard A. <u>Debris of Battle: The Wounded of Gettysburg.</u> Mechanicsburg, PA. Stackpole Books. 1997.

Small, Cindy L. <u>The Jenny Wade Story: A True and Complete Account of the Only Civilian Killed During the Battle of Gettysburg.</u> Gettysburg, PA. Thomas Publications. 1991.

Websites:

www.campletterman.org
www.civilwarmed.org/prosthetics/
www.library.bowdoin.edu/arch/archives/msmg.shtml
www.stfxcc.org/hospital
www.thepeopleshistory.com

CPSIA information can be obtained
at www.ICGtesting.com
Printed in the USA
LVHW090745010720
659398LV00003BA/338